MUDDY WATER

Shadows of Camelot Crossing

A Haunting in Stillwater, Book 3

LISA COURTAWAY

LISA COURTAWAY

MUDDY WATER

SHADOWS OF CAMELOT CROSSING
A HAUNTING IN STILLWATER BOOK 3

ISBN: 978-1-7374222-6-6 (ebook)

ISBN: 978-1-7374222-7-3 (print)

Editing and Formatting by Two Birds Author Services

www.twobirdsauthorservices.com

Cover Design by Miblart

www.miblart.com

Dedicated to my amazing children,
Connor, Caleb, Reed and Zoe.
You are my heart and soul
and always come first.

Author's Note

This book contains subject matter related to abortion.

A deceit so potent it could lay waste to lineages
A tiny seed ruined before life could spring forth
A pretense well crafted in a faithless smile

No length too great to protect the guilty
No act forbidden to preserve constructs
No mistakes left uncovered to rattle the front

The fatherless daughter both sinner and saint
The rival and martyr surrenders her soul
The kinship remorseless cinching deceit

Of countless casualties one voice rings loud
Of sublime rage hastened by a lifetime of neglect
Of fear hails atrocities driven by shame

For the wraith who seeks witness will be denied
For one who has answers a tenet is formed
For the sake of an outsider too dire the toll

So confidences held
So ties unraveled
So voices quieted

Verity departs along with breath

Prologue

"Welcome to *What Would Dad Say?* Here's your host, Cliff Weston!"

"Hello and welcome!" Cliff Weston sprinted onto the stage. "Let's meet today's players: Contestant number one—"

"Hi, Cliff! My name is Mindy Fugate, and I'm from Park City, Utah!"

"Nice to have you here today, Mindy. Contestant number two?"

"I'm Roger Norris, and I'm from Chicago, Illinois!"

"Welcome, Roger! And last but not least, contestant number three."

Carly froze. She had been dropped inside a pinball machine. The lights and bells were dizzying. She did not know how she'd ended up here, but was aware she was contestant number three because she stood next to Roger Norris. Roger looked at her with a plastered smile. Its intensity made her cheeks ache. *I'd never be a contestant on a game show*, she thought.

"Contestant number three, please tell us your name and where you are from." The host glared at her over his cue cards.

"Um, Carly Bennett, S-S-Stillwater, Oklahoma." The

words tangled on her tongue, then came spilling out before she could clasp her hand over her mouth.

"Wonderful! You know the game..."

No, I don't know the game, Cliff! Carly thought. It was the only sentence she could string together in her state of confusion. Her hand remained fixed to her face. Fortunately for her, the spirited Mr. Weston stepped up to fill in a few of the blanks that hung over her head like a thick fog.

"I'll ask you questions about your dad, and when you know the answer, hit your buzzer..."

Carly looked down at her hand. Gripped tightly in her fist was a device she didn't recognize. Without thinking, she pushed the button and jumped when the buzzer vibrated in her grasp and a nearby loudspeaker screamed at her.

"Oh, too quick on the draw there, Carly. You've got to wait until I ask a question." The man's gleaming white teeth clenched and while he maintained his composure, each sentence ended in an upturned pitch. It was apparent to Carly he was losing patience.

The audience—that until now she'd been unaware of—erupted in laughter. Her face was as red as the button on the buzzer. Heat built in her body like a pressure cooker, escaping in tiny droplets of sweat beading under her nose and at her temples.

"Each answer you give correctly is worth two hundred points. But be careful! If your answer doesn't match your dad's response, you lose one hundred points and you'll hear this." Mark pointed to the sky and Carly glanced up. A labyrinth of catwalks and ropes dipped out of the blackness.

A harsh alarm blasted, and Carly flinched as the audience applauded wildly.

"The player with the highest score heads to the final round with their dad for a chance at the jackpot!"

"Wait, my, my father is here?" Carly questioned, leaning into the microphone to be heard over the roar of the crowd.

She turned in a circle, the cord to the buzzer wrapping around her. Eyes squinted against the harsh lights, Carly desperately scanned the area, searching for her father. Cliff ignored her question, but Mindy shot her a caustic look while Roger hissed through clenched teeth.

"Get with the program, Carly," Roger said. His smile never faltered, despite the venom in his tone.

Carly spun in the other direction, fighting with the buzzer cord until she was free of it and facing the host again. She nodded at Roger apologetically, immediately angered by the speed at which she conformed to the wants of a complete stranger.

Cliff Weston slid a finger between his neck and shirt collar and pulled; a nervous chuckle slid out of his mouth.

"Okay, first question: what is your dad's favorite holiday?"

The buzzer screamed again, but this time it was for Roger. A wave of relief washed over Carly.

"Player number two: your dad's favorite holiday."

"Easy one, Cliff: Halloween."

"Let's see what Roger's pop had to say about his favorite holiday."

The stage went dark. On a screen above Cliff's head, an older version of Roger appeared. Carly took advantage of the lighting shift to hazard a glance into the audience. Row after row of smiling people filled the seats, their numbers infinite. The room spun, forcing her to look away.

"My favorite holiday? That's an easy one: Halloween," middle-aged Roger answered.

Again, the crowd roared with applause while a dinging bell attempted to blot them out.

"Right on! That's two hundred points for Roger! Next question: what's your dad's favorite song? Your dad's favorite—"

The buzzer buzzed, this time for Mindy.

"Oh, gosh, it's a toss-up," Mindy said, her eyes shifting

back and forth as if she were trying to choose which cheeseburger she would order off an invisible menu.

"Twenty seconds, Mindy. We need your answer."

A hush rippled through the audience.

"Oh, gosh, 'Rhinestone Cowboy?'" Her tone rose in doubt.

"'Rhinestone Cowboy.' Let's see what Mr. Fugate has to say about his favorite song."

The stage lights went black again, and another man appeared on the screen.

"My favorite song? Huh, that's a tough one. I'd say either 'Country Roads'..."

The crowd played along, gasping as if Mindy's dad were teetering on a ledge about to jump.

"No, no, 'Rhinestone Cowboy'–that's it, my absolute favorite song."

Mindy's dad disappeared from the screen and Mindy bounced up and down, awkwardly clapping with the buzzer in her hand. Roger leaned over and high-fived her.

"Next question: what's your dad's favorite movie? Dad's favorite movie."

Carly squared her shoulders and straightened her spine, adding two inches of height to her frame. Unsure of where this uncharacteristically competitive edge came from, her game face emerged and her eyes grew wide. *I know this one!* Her hand tightened on the buzzer as her mind struggled with what to do. The buzzer screamed, and she prepared to blurt out the answer.

"My dad's favorite movie..."

"Oh, sorry, Carly—Roger beat you to the buzzer. If he gets it wrong, you'll get your chance."

Carly closed her eyes and held her breath. If she didn't get to answer this question, she'd never get on the scoreboard. She had no clue what her father's favorite food or beer or car was. But she knew his favorite movie. How she'd gained that knowledge was a mystery to her, but she was certain she'd get it right.

"This one is a cinch, Mark. My dad's favorite movie is *Star Wars*."

Please be wrong, please be wrong … Carly crossed her fingers.

"Show us what Mr. Norris said his favorite movie is."

Mr. Norris's smiling face appeared on the screen. He did the best Chewbacca impression Carly'd ever heard.

"*Star Wars!*"

"Good job, Roger! You are in the lead by two hundred points!"

This time Mindy held her hand up for a high-five, but Roger was too busy fist-pumping to notice. The audience loved it.

Defeated, Carly dropped her buzzer. She glimpsed herself on a monitor. What stood out to her more than the three flashing zeros under her name was her attire. She was wearing her pajamas, her long brown hair tied up in a messy bun. A mustard stain stood out on her light-gray hoodie, remnants of the sandwich she ate for dinner. Her body shrank as she tried to hide behind the podium. Roger and Mindy were dressed smartly, no mustard stains, no stains at all.

"Oh, Carly, you need to get in the game! You're trailing by two hundred points!"

Thanks for the heads-up, Cliff. Her attention now focused squarely on letting her hair down and fixing it to cover the bright yellow smudge.

"Get those buzzers ready, contestants, and tell us what your dad's favorite color is, his favorite color." Cliff looked each contestant in the eyes. Roger and Mindy searched their minds, brows furrowing and heads tilting. Roger's gaze shifted up, while Mindy's glanced downward as she mouthed the words "favorite color" repeatedly.

Carly saw her chance and took it, snatching the buzzer back in her left hand and bopping with her right.

"Carly, here's your chance to get on the board! Your dad's favorite color."

Reality smacked Carly in the face. She had no clue what her father's favorite color was, or if he even had a favorite color. She went with the most obvious answer that flashed through her mind. Her father was a man of power. Power men liked red.

"Red!" she blurted out, a smile stretched across her face. She puffed out her chest, mustard stain be damned.

"Red. Let's see if Mr. Bennett's favorite color is red."

Carly was taken aback by the sight of her father when his face popped up on the screen. She was mesmerized by how old he looked. His face bore no smile. His eyes darted about. He appeared to be as shocked by his locale as Carly was. A voice off camera whispered.

"Your favorite color, sir—"

"Right, um, I give little time to thoughts of my favorite color, but my wife buys me blue everything. Blue shirts, blue pants, blue undershorts..."

The crowd got a kick out of that one, and laughter rolled like a wave through the studio.

"So, yeah, I'll bet my life on blue. My favorite color is blue."

The entire space deflated with a despondent gasp, and the loudest buzzer of all exploded. Carly recoiled and covered her head with a pillow. The buzzer didn't stop until her hand reached out from under the covers and groped her nightstand, finally landing on her phone.

As she swiped the green bar on the phone, she noted the caller was her sister, Liv. Before Liv spoke one word, she knew her father was dead.

"Carly, I'm so sorry to wake you in the middle of the night. It's Father. He's gone."

Liv was too distraught to share details at three o'clock in the morning, and Carly was too tired to absorb anything. The din of the game show dream still echoed in her head. Floaters flashed before her eyes from the array of phantom lights. The call had saved her from drowning in the surreal weirdness of the dream. Their conversation was brief, with a promise to speak again in a few hours.

Carly yanked the blankets up around her ears, waking Clovis. The cat made his way to her face, pawing at the blankets for entry to a warmer spot where he could curl up and doze off again. Carly hoped for a few more hours of sleep, but the news of Father's passing made that impossible. Thoughts of what the loss of the enigmatic man might mean to the family, to her mostly, roiled through her mind. There were no tears; she felt no sadness.

A trip to Stillwater would be required. She'd be expected to attend her father's funeral, though she hadn't seen or spoken to the man in a year or two. She didn't want to face her hometown, stepmother, half-siblings, and the cost of the trip. As she lay in bed, eyes wide-open, memories of the trippy dream were pushed aside by visions of the turmoil she would face in the coming days.

She didn't see her father take a seat in the threadbare papasan chair in the corner of her tiny room. While she didn't notice his first visitation, Carly Bennett began seeing more of her father after he passed than she ever had while he was alive.

Chapter One

2022

The sun settled low in the Arizona sky, then slipped below the snow-capped summit of Humphrey's Peak, conceding to the moon and its nightly respite from the blazing desert sun. Four hours into her fifteen-hour drive, things were going well. Traffic was light. The tense roller-coaster passage through the San Francisco Mountain Range was behind her, and Carly was optimistic the night drive would be uneventful. She'd always loved road trips; there was something cathartic in chasing down the yellow line, singing at the top of her lungs. This trip didn't hold the promise of a good time. Her father's funeral was something she'd never given thought to. Now it snatched up every free second her mind had.

Going home had never been kind to her. It was easier to forget the past in Tempe. She promised herself long ago that she would break free of her stifling existence in Stillwater, Oklahoma, as quickly as she could. The desert sun was what she needed; anonymity was what she needed more.

She eased her car on to I-40 as the sky fell full-dark. The

headlights allowed her the only glimpse of the future she could cope with.

The miles blurred by, and the night grew blacker with the absence of streetlights. She stopped a few times to fill up her tank and her coffee mug. Traveling through the dark hours was easier, more solitary, the way she liked it.

During her final hours in the state of Texas, fatigue was wearing on her. Carly cranked up the stereo, hoping a lively sing-along would perk her up. The first notes of "Piece by Piece" began. *Ironic,* she thought, inhaling deeply before belting out the words she knew by heart; a song that cut so deeply it often brought tears to her eyes.

She didn't cry this time as she sang along. The familiar tune lulled her mind when suddenly the music stopped. It took her a few beats to realize the stereo had gone silent while she continued bellowing the words of a song that embodied much of what Carly believed was wrong with her.

Daring to take her eyes off the road, she saw the stereo had shut off. She jabbed the *power* button and waited for the song to continue, focusing again on the road ahead, noticing the abundant insect carnage on her windshield.

The Kelly Clarkson song did not come back, but she instantly recognized the opening guitar riff of Everclear's notable song about an absentee father. The cycle of music reached one of her favorite playlists, the one she'd named "Daddy Issues."

"Fitting," Carly said to the empty car.

She cranked the volume up and sang along, drumming her thumbs on the steering wheel. Again, in mid-play, the song went silent.

"Come on," she pleaded with the stereo, punching the *power* button once more. "We're almost there."

A semi blew by her in the passing lane. Its air horn made her jump, and she yanked the steering wheel, steadying her car. Before this loud reminder that others shared the road with her, her car had been drifting.

"Sorry!" she yelled as the lights of the truck disappeared over a small incline.

She checked her mirrors and didn't detect any other vehicle lights before returning her attention to the stereo. A song started right up, but this time she remained quiet, though it was one of her favorites. She listened to "Styrofoam Plates" without singing along. The song played to its end. She held her breath awaiting the next song, one of her all-time favorites, "Top of the World." She was powerless to keep from singing along, but she did so softly without the passion the tune usually inspired in her.

Like the anticipation of musical chairs, she wasn't surprised this time when the song abruptly stopped. At the same time, an overwhelming smell invaded her nose. Its familiarity was dizzying, and for a moment, all she could do was focus on not getting sick behind the wheel of the car. Gathering herself, she pushed a button and the passenger front window slid down. The night air rushed in, but it did nothing to drive away the aroma, one she would forever recognize as the scent of her father. It was a heady mix of Givenchy Gentleman and Irish Spring soap fighting for their place against the smell of cigarette smoke. Her father had quit smoking years ago, but she would never forget his scent. Bile rose in her throat and she choked it down. She jerked the steering wheel to the right and came to a sudden stop on the shoulder, the wheels skidding over debris before finding grip.

Carly turned her hazard lights on and rolled down the back windows. The driver's side window wouldn't lower after something in the door broke several months before. She'd never bothered getting it fixed. Rolling windows down in Tempe was uncommon. The rare visit to a drive-thru restaurant was awkward, but not enough to prompt her to cough up the money to fix it. Now she wished she'd had it taken care of, as she felt the need to purify the air.

During her struggles with the sound system, she'd lost track of the miles she left behind. A sign ahead caught in her high beams and drew her back, and the nauseating aroma permeating the interior subsided. There were still hours to go before sunrise. The darkness that once brought comfort was now menacing. She rummaged through her tote bag and pulled out some Sour Skittles, her favorite road trip snack. Before getting back on the highway, she selected a podcast she hoped would hold her interest for the rest of the drive.

Weariness settled upon her as she crossed the border into Oklahoma. She prepared to tap her horn at the sign welcoming her to her home state, when motion caught her attention. Fearing a deer or nocturnal animal was lurking too close to the road, she eased off the gas pedal, slowing considerably. There were no other travelers sharing this stretch of interstate with her. What moved in the dim light of the roadside sign was no animal. It was far too tall and was waving an arm. A voice in her head sounded an alarm, imploring her to drive on. That voice drowned out the ingrained Oklahoma hospitality telling her she couldn't leave a person abandoned on the side of the highway in the wee hours of the morning.

She dropped her speed to nearly a crawl, hoping to assess the situation more clearly by seeing who the person was. What if it was a child or a woman? Could she bring herself to lend a hand? She knew better.

The person stepped onto the road, and the car's headlights washed over them. The sight hit Carly like a punch to the stomach. It was a man. He was wearing a business suit and was smiling and waving as if he had not a care in the world. It was Mitch Bennett, her dead father.

She clenched her eyes closed, and a startled but weak yelp escaped her throat as she swerved to avoid hitting him. Her entire body tensed, locking her arms. The car swayed and she forced herself to right the vehicle before it careened into the ditch. If she lost control and wrecked, she'd be stuck out here in the dark with her dead father. At this hour, there were almost no cars on the highway. Taking deep breaths to calm herself, she hazarded a glance in the rearview mirror. There was no one there.

Picking up her speed, but still panicky, she dug through her bag for an energy drink she kept there in case she ever struggled to stay awake while driving. Without a doubt, this situation called for the surge of caffeine. Fatigue had caused her to hallucinate. That was the only plausible explanation she could come up with. She drove on, chugging the bitter drink in three large gulps. The effects of the drink jolted her, and jitters replaced sleepiness.

To stay alert and focused, she counted roadkill, making a game out of the animal carcasses she passed. She implemented an impromptu scoring system based on the size and rarity of animals who fell victim to the highway. It was all she could think to do to settle her nerves. Her score rose exponentially as she neared her hometown.

Chapter Two

2002

"You sit right by that window and don't take your eyes off of it," Mother instructed Carly. "I don't want to catch a glimpse of that man, so you hop up and scoot out before he even pulls into the driveway."

"I know," Carly replied.

Carly leaned against the long narrow window by the front door. Her duffle bag lay at her feet. Mother sat in the recliner, a cigarette in hand, legs crossed, one swinging restlessly. A tattered house shoe threatened to fall off with each kick.

"Olivia Ann Bennett! You best get your tush out here right now! Your father will be here any minute."

"Coming," Liv called.

"Why do we even have to go? I don't want to spend my weekend in a hospital room with Chip," Carly whined. She calculated the hours of boredom she and her sister would suffer stuck at the bedside of their ailing half-brother. Adding to the struggle would be their stepmother, Janace, who would tirelessly fuss over the boy. The total was dreadful, ending up somewhere between endless and infinity.

"Yeah, well, you can take that up with your father. He's skipped out on your visitations two times in a row. Serves him right having to take the two of you this weekend."

"You could've just canceled," Liv added as she entered the living room.

"Could have, but didn't. Mothers need me-time too. One of the many things Mitch Bennett doesn't understand is how hard it is raising kids all by yourself."

"He's here," Carly announced, grabbing her bag, turning to make sure Liv had hers.

Shrugging her backpack on, Liv stopped and fanned away the cloud of smoke encircling Mother's head before kissing her cheek. Mother batted at the girl, shooing her away.

"Bye. Love you. Don't miss us too much," Liv said, running the few steps to the door.

"Wait! I need you both to remember. You don't call him Daddy anymore. He gave up that name. He's your father now; that's what you call him."

"We know," Liv replied, slumping her shoulders and rolling her eyes. "We know."

"Okay then. Get on out of here. And give him hell," Mother shouted as Liv closed the door.

A light drizzle fell, setting the tone for a miserable weekend.

The window rolled down on the driver's side of the car.

"You girls hustle! Your brother and Janace need some stuff up at the hospital. I don't have all day."

The girls picked up their pace and sprinted to the car.

"Shotgun!" Liv yelled, whizzing past Carly.

Liv got in the front seat and tossed her backpack behind her, hitting Carly in the head as she climbed into the BMW. Neither girl spoke as their father backed out of the driveway. Carly glanced up to see her mother standing in the window.

"Sorry this weekend won't work out the way we'd hoped.

Your brother is in quite a bit of pain, but the surgery went well. We hope to take him home tomorrow."

The girls nodded.

"Pretty bad run of luck for the poor kid. Getting his first football injury when he's barely five years old. He doesn't want to talk about the injury or the surgery, so be mindful. The whole deal is a little sensitive, especially to a boy his age."

Father turned up the radio, and soon Carly was quietly singing along. As the chorus started, she turned toward the window, keeping her voice to herself when the radio went silent. A hot flush rose on her face as she realized she was singing with no radio to hide her voice.

"Come on, girl, keep singing. You got a real nice voice."

Father's eyes locked on Carly's from the rearview mirror. Carly couldn't think of anything to say and wondered if her father saw the fiery blush on her cheeks. All she could muster was a weak chuckle.

"I like that song," Liv said. "Turn it back on."

"And now, 'These Days' by Rascal Flatts," the radio announcer said, introducing the next song.

Without thinking, Carly started singing along. In the middle of the chorus, the radio fell silent again. This time Carly was too into the song and continued for several lines before she heard Liv snicker.

"He got you again, Carly. She hates it when you do that, you know."

"Well, it's the only way I can hear her pipes. You know, when you were born, I thought, this one has a set of lungs on her. I mean, yeah, you cried a lot. But there was something told me you'd be a singer. Kind of thought it might happen by now, you know. You'd be one of those Disney kids or something. Guess there's still time, though. But if you're gonna be a singer, you gotta let people hear you sing."

"That's why I sing in the choir, so my voice blends in with

everyone else. But my music teacher said I'd be a shoo-in for Madrigal when I get to high school. Said I should take voice lessons."

"Voice lessons? What do you need voice lessons for when you can sing already?"

"I don't know, improve my range, maybe boost my confidence..."

"Nonsense. No need throwing good money at something you can do naturally. If your voice is as good as she says it is, don't figure you need lessons."

Carly shrugged and shifted her gaze back to the view outside. Mother had scoffed at the idea of vocal training as well.

"Here we are. What do you say we stop at the gift shop and pick up a little something for your brother?"

Carly and Liv mumbled agreements as they got out of the car. Mitch took his windbreaker off and covered his head, jogging out in front of the girls. Once he reached the covered awning at the hospital entrance, he put his jacket back on and waved at them to hurry.

Chip's hospital room was down a long, brightly colored hallway. A few kids in robes, clutching IV poles, ambled through the halls. Snippets of television shows slipped into the corridor from darkened rooms. Somewhere close by, an infant wailed angrily, drowning out the dings and clatter of medical equipment and ringing telephones.

The girls followed dutifully behind their father. Sitting atop his shoulder was the face of a child-sized teddy bear dressed in a football uniform, complete with dark smudges under his eyes. It ogled the girls with crazed googly eyes that bobbed madly.

Mitch reached the door before the girls and turned to shush them, putting a finger to his lips. The move was pointless, as neither Carly nor Liv were making a sound. He tapped lightly on the door.

"Knock, knock," Mitch said in a deep, growly voice. He held the football bear in front of his face as he pushed the door open with his foot. "Look who I found in the hallway! They've come to cheer you up."

The room was dim. Balloons emblazoned with Get Well bobbed and swayed, enlivened by the air conditioning vents on the ceiling. Carly had never seen so many bouquets outside a florist's shop. Chip looked tiny, asleep in the bed. Machines behind him flashed and ticked.

"Hush, now, Mitch Bennett," Janace whispered, rising from a chair near the bed. "He's just drifted off. Don't wake him. They finally gave him something to ease his pain. Poor boy was in tears."

Janace stood on her tiptoes and kissed Mitch on the cheek.

"Who's this big guy?" she asked, plucking the bear out of Mitch's hands. "Surely you girls didn't get this for him, did you?" Janace hugged the bear. Her gaze never fell on Carly or Liv.

"Well, they helped me pick it out down in the gift shop. Right, girls?" Mitch gave Carly a conspiratorial wink and walked to the bed where he brushed Chip's hair from his forehead.

Liv circled the small space. Her fingers danced over each vase and she stopped to breathe deeply, inhaling the fragrance of each arrangement. Janace swatted at her stepdaughter without taking her eyes off the football teddy bear.

"I'm sure he'll love it when it he's feeling better."

Someone knocked on the door before entering the room without waiting for a response. Seeing that it was the doctor, Janace straightened her shirt and pinched her cheeks. The woman didn't have makeup on. Carly couldn't remember a time when she'd seen Janace with a clean face.

"Mr. and Mrs. Bennett, how's our patient doing?" the doctor asked as he grabbed a clipboard hanging from the bed and reviewed it.

"Girls, do you mind? Go wait in the hall while we talk to the doctor," Janace said as she nudged Carly's shoulder.

The girls exited, but curiosity nagged at Carly. She knew Chip was hurt during football practice. All seemed well, as practice continued, but by the time they got home Chip was writhing in pain. Janace took him to the emergency room, and they'd performed surgery. On what part of his body, Carly didn't know. There was no cast on his leg nor visible bandages giving any hints.

Liv started to say something, but Carly shushed her and leaned her ear close to the door. Janace hadn't closed it all the way.

"Well, the surgery went well, and the nurses tell me they've got his pain controlled. Do you have any questions?"

"Yes, doctor, I … well, I don't know how to ask this question, but we're wondering if this will, well, you know..." Janace's words drifted off.

"She wants to know if this is going to affect his swimmers, Doc."

"Oh, um, yes, well, there's really no way of knowing right now. That's something we'll have to look at a bit later. Right now, I'd say he's doing as best as can be expected. If all goes well, I think we can release him tomorrow."

"Thank you so much, Doctor," Janace replied in a sugar-coated voice.

Things quieted down inside the room as Carly tried to process the meaning of the conversation. She had no idea what her father meant by swimmers. Chip started playing football in the peewee division shortly after he'd mastered walking. He'd never been a swimmer aside from the swimming pool at their father's home.

Too busy pondering what happened to her half-brother, she didn't take notice of the doctor making his way to the door. He almost collided with her as he exited.

"Excuse me," Carly whispered, her face flushed, and she couldn't meet the doctor's eyes.

Mitch met the girls in the hallway.

"What say we head down to the cafeteria and rustle up some food for Janace? The poor woman hasn't eaten a thing today. Maybe your brother will be awake when we come back up."

Chapter Three

2022

Perhaps the buzz of the energy drink still coursed through her body, or she was more road-weary than she thought, or maybe it was due to the disturbances she'd encountered on the long drive, but Carly drove straight past the Roadside Motel. She didn't acknowledge the detour until she found her car sitting in front of the small duplex where she and Liv grew up. She rolled the three working windows down and breathed in the crisp morning air. Oklahoma had a freshness that Tempe couldn't mimic.

She killed the engine, closed her eyes and inhaled deeply. The unmistakable scent of wild onion reached her nose first. Spring was inching its way into Stillwater. In a nearby tree, a mourning dove practiced its owl impersonation, and drops of heavy dew glistened in the light of the early morning. Murky, gray clouds hovered in the distance, threatening to blot out the sun soon. She was always struck by the vibrant array of hues in Oklahoma. The ever-changing medley of sky, greenery, wildflowers, and dirt, forsaken in the arid desert where an unchanging palette of muted earth tones was the norm. While

Arizona found a different beauty in the monochromatic, the Oklahoma kaleidoscope was brilliant.

Not much had changed since she'd lived there with her mother and sister. The wood and trim had been painted a lighter shade of brown. On the wall near the door, one of the house numbers sat askew, and the driveway was oil-stained.

She wondered about the people who lived in the dingy duplex now and hoped they were happier than she and her sister had been. A small bicycle lay in the yard, one wheel turning slowly in the gentle breeze. Carly watched it spin and drifted back to her youth. Her mind tried to stop her, a part warning her to move on, get to the hotel, sleep. The other part won, the one that spoke like a ghost reliving a hellish event.

Chapter Four

2001

Carly found herself face-down on the hot asphalt. An echoing ring in her ears silenced the world to her confused mind. The first noise to break through the resounding peal was a yapping dog. She was eye-to-eye with a small mutt. The barking yielded to a voice that pushed through the clamorous buzz. A shadow moved over her like a cloud.

"Oh my," the voice said. "Are you okay?"

The stranger's question became a distant memory as shock and numbness gave way to throbbing pain. In her mind, she ran through everything that hurt. She could not determine where the worst pain came from: face, nose, mouth, or hand. A coppery brine filled her mouth. There was a tooth lying next to her on the pavement. She allowed her tongue to feel its way around her mouth; filaments of tattered skin spilled blood. There it was, a gap, upper front. The tooth was hers. *Obviously I'm not okay,* she thought from her face-down position in the middle of the neighborhood street.

"Let me help you up. Do you think you can stand?" the unfamiliar voice said. It was a woman. The stranger's dark shape eclipsed the sun, her features obscured in a blinding aura.

Reluctantly, Carly spat before attempting to respond. "Yeah, I think." Her words were unrecognizable even to herself, lisping, like her mouth was full of cotton balls. She wondered for a flash how many cotton balls it would take to clean this mess, when her thoughts shifted with a sudden jolt, her muddled mind clearing enough now to comprehend. Behind clenched eyes, she envisioned herself smiling with a missing front tooth. A choking cry burst out of her, spewing crimson droplets. Physical pain dimmed to the searing sting of one horrible thought, going through life missing a front tooth, which she now found in her right palm.

The woman reached out a hand to Carly, but quickly withdrew it. Carly caught sight of her arm as it floated away from her toward the woman and understood the woman's hesitancy. A fiery, raw road rash scored her lightly freckled skin. Carly was grateful the stranger resisted offering help, sparing her the pain of a grasp.

A perturbed toddler sat in a stroller, kicking his feet dangerously close to her ravaged face, so she pushed through the pain of movement, and rose shakily. The dog seemed more upset than the restless boy. It continued to yip, defying its owner's orders to stop.

"Roscoe, quiet," the woman said as she let go of the stroller to help Carly right her bike. Carly stood, causing fresh drops of blood to spill onto the pavement. The stranger flinched as her face came into Carly's view. It was apparent she was attempting to balance her eagerness to help with her desire to avoid being showered by the young girl's messy sobs.

The landscape flip-flopped and color dimmed to an inky gray as dizziness threatened to flatten her again. Carly faltered and hesitated, waiting for color and stability to return, before she was able to form a coherent reply to the next question asked of her.

"Where do you live, sweetie? Do you think we can walk there?"

Unable to trust her voice, she nodded before being seized by another surge of tears. Carly took her bike from the stranger, keeping the tooth gripped tightly in her unmarred hand, and saw the cause of this disaster. Her roller skates hung over the handlebars of her Schwinn where she had placed them in the ill-fated attempt to bring both sets of wheels home. Lisey's mom had reminded her to take her skates as she bound out of her friend's door. She couldn't remember exactly when she had left the skates at Lisey's house, but knew it was weeks ago. One wheel of the skates was now tangled in the twisted spokes of the bike's front tire. She lifted the front of the bike, freeing the back wheel to roll unimpeded.

The early spring sun glared down from the Oklahoma sky as the group made the short trek to Carly's house. They walked in awkward silence. The stranger followed Carly's lead to the end of the driveway. There, Carly dropped the bike and turned to the stranger, hoping her damaged face could convey her gratitude, before dashing to the weather-worn front door. Hurt now awakened in her shins. Her white Keds were spattered with bright red spots. She paused for a moment at the door, turning again to give a feeble wave. Roscoe was intently sniffing the cracked wooden base of the mailbox. The stranger raised her hand in return as the toddler protested another unscheduled stop, kicking his sandaled feet, interrupting the woman's gesture. Never completing the wave, the stranger returned her hand to the stroller, gave Roscoe's leash a tug, and hurried down the street.

"Mother!" Carly screamed as she threw the door open, leaving a bloody, smeared handprint on the knob. Inside the house, the pain now fully realized, adrenaline pulsed through her again and panic body-slammed her. She needed an adult to make decisions, to help her. In a deep part of her young mind, a voice fought to be heard. It told her the one adult she had to depend on would likely not live up to the task. "Mother!" she screamed again, searching the duplex on shaky legs, being mindful to not get blood on the faded shag carpet.

"Keep your voice down, Carly!" Mother yelled as she came out of the bathroom, drying her hands on her washed-out black sweatpants.

At the same time, her sister, Liv, ran inside from the backyard. Carly opened her hand, revealing the tooth, and was hit with the disbelief that a tooth that large could fit inside the small gap it was forced out of. Her mother gasped, and Liv caught sight of the object in Carly's palm. The young girl burst into wailing tears more intense than even Carly's, her breath fast and halting.

"What happened to you?" Mother shouted, working herself into a frenzy. "Liv, get my keys and my purse!"

Tears cutting lines through the dirt on her face, Liv did as she was told, and somehow—the voice of reason at the age of seven—also grabbed a dish towel, filled it with ice cubes and handed it to Carly. Mother was a flurry of disorganized energy, looking for her shoes, working her fingers through her hair, and talking to herself.

"Why do these things always happen to me?" They rarely did. In fact, this was the first time either of her children had busted their face open by falling off their bike. Liv did break her arm at school once, and Carly supposed that's what Mother was talking about.

"I don't have time for this. I've got work in the morning." Of course, no one ever really had time for things like this, and Carly had school in the morning too; so did Liv. Carly wondered what she would look like in the morning. The image provoked another wave of blubbering sobs that took her breath away.

"How am I going to pay for this?" Carly didn't have a comeback, even in her head, for that question.

Amid the tears and chaos, Liv took Carly by the arm and helped her to the car. She reached across Carly, seemingly untroubled by her sister's bloodied clothes, and buckled the seat belt. Next, Liv freed a tangle of hair stuck in the drying goo on Carly's cheek and tucked it behind her sister's ear. Then she gently guided Carly's hand that held the ice pack to her face before climbing into the back seat.

On the ten-minute drive east to Stillwater Medical Center, Carly tried her best to explain what happened. It wasn't easy. The swelling in her mouth was increasing, the pain becoming unbearable. She was powerless to control her hitching moans, making the telling more difficult. By the time they arrived at the ER parking lot, Mother had pieced enough of a story together to explain the situation to the woman at the desk. The receptionist was unfazed. A child with a bloody, swollen face was all in a day's work for the unflappable professional. Mother made it obvious she didn't appreciate the woman's calm demeanor. It was a crisis for her, so everyone should panic.

Liv helped Carly to a bank of pink, molded plastic seats as far as possible from the others waiting for care. Their mother waged an unnecessary battle with the receptionist. Mother didn't have her insurance card and didn't want to be bothered with the paperwork. The receptionist pointed to where Carly and Liv sat. A nurse called Carly's name before Mother had a chance to sit. The nurse held a door open for them as Liv helped Carly cross the room.

The young nurse ushered them to a curtained bed. She was gentle with Carly and exhibited a patience with Mother that made Carly grateful, introducing herself as Nurse Patsy and listening as Mother described the events. She got almost all the details incorrect and was already embellishing the way she always did, making herself seem blameless and more sympathetic. Carly didn't know why her mother was retelling the story this way. It wasn't Mother's fault. Carly was the dufus who hung her skates over the handlebars.

Nurse Patsy took Carly's vitals, jotted some notes and then shone a bright light in Carly's face, pulling back the wet, bloody muck of the dishrag.

"Well, you did right with the ice pack," she said.

Mother nodded her head emphatically, taking credit for the act.

"You certainly did a number on your beautiful face. Knocked that tooth clean out, root and all," Nurse Patsy said calmly. "Don't you worry. Dr. Carter is on the way. He'll have you looking as pretty as ever in no time." She carefully plucked the tooth from Carly's hand. "I'm going to put this in a special solution to clean it and keep it fresh. Hopefully, Dr. Carter can pop it right back into where it came from."

Carly wanted to ask what happened if he couldn't, but her mouth felt ten times bigger than normal, making it impossible for her to speak. She nodded, the tears running down the sides of her face, pooling in her ears in cold puddles as she lay in the bright light. The what-ifs were more overwhelming than the pain.

"Now, you are going to be fine. I promise." There they were, the reassuring words Carly needed to hear. Nurse Patsy continued, "The attending is putting orders in for something that will help with the pain while we wait for Dr. Carter. You poor dear. I'll be right back." She returned quickly and draped a warm blanket over Carly. Her next action released some pent-up tension Carly didn't realize she was feeling: Nurse Patsy took a second blanket and wrapped it around Liv, gently lifting her long, golden hair out of the blanket and smoothing it. "You have such gorgeous hair," she cooed. "I bet you're hungry. I can bring you a snack. What do you like best, grape juice or apple juice?"

Liv looked to Mother, and Carly could tell Nurse Patsy

sensed the dilemma. "They are complimentary. It might be a long night."

Mother gave a nod.

"Apple juice, please." Liv's voice was barely a whisper.

"Is there someplace I can have a smoke?" Mother blurted. "My nerves are shot."

"Head back up to the front desk. The receptionist can point the way. This little one can stay here," Nurse Patsy said, patting Liv's head. "I'll be right back with those pain meds, some juice, and graham crackers. Don't go anywhere, you two," she said with a wink.

Mother pushed past Nurse Patsy before the nurse turned to leave.

Dr. Carter was able to put Carly's tooth back in the void left when her face collided with the pavement. Carly's awareness waned, drifting in and out of a twilight sleep, as he spent two hours doing his best to right her damaged face. Aside from the tooth being knocked out, her bottom teeth punched a hole in her face just below her lower lip. Dr. Carter stitched inside her mouth, while a few more delicate stitches closed the skin on her chin.

Finally, he clamped on thick, heavy braces to hold the tooth in place until her body healed and accepted its missing piece. They weren't the braces kids wore at school with the colorful bands and rubber bands that tugged awkwardly when they smiled but looked kind of cool, like a preteen rite of passage. These braces were clunky vices that bonded to her teeth, gripping them painfully. There was no concern for aesthetics or comfort. When the doctor finished, he informed Mother that he wanted to admit her overnight. Carly kept her eyes closed and felt as if she were spying on the doctor and her mother. She couldn't contain the tears that slipped down her face. Even at her young age, she knew an overnight stay in a hospital would cost a lot.

"She indicates she may have lost consciousness, if only

briefly. It's safest if we keep her here and monitor her for twenty-four hours to make sure she doesn't have a concussion," the doctor said.

"Is it really necessary to spend the night? What if I just checked on her from time-to-time while she's sleeping?"

"Sorry, ma'am. I think it's best that she stay here." Turning to Carly, he added, "No need to worry, young lady. There are worse things than a night in the hospital."

Carly figured the doctor thought her tears were tears of pain or fear about a hospital stay. He was wrong. She wished he had agreed to send her home.

"Nurse Patsy will be in to move you up to your room soon. I"ll come by and check on you tomorrow morning, and if all goes well, I will spring you in the evening. Look on the bright side. You'll get to eat all the ice cream you can over the next week or so." Dr. Carter smiled at Carly, then turned and left.

"Well, this is just great. Why couldn't you have been more careful, Carly? I'm going to have to call your father to see if you can stay with him tonight, Liv."

Liv had almost fallen asleep, but her mother's words jolted her awake, and she began crying again in fear. Neither she nor Liv had spent many nights at their father and stepmother's house, and they certainly had never done so without the other.

"No! I want to stay here with Carly. Please!" Liv pleaded, shaking her head.

"I'm sure it's against some hospital policy, but I guess it won't hurt to ask. It'd save me from having to deal with him, or Janace." She rifled through her purse, and when she found her lighter, pulled back the curtain and looked both directions. "I'll go see if I can find someone to ask about you staying," she said, closing the curtain. Her shadow disappeared down the corridor.

Liv approached her sister cautiously, as if afraid her mere presence would do harm.

"Ouch! That looks like it hurts bad. I'm so sorry, Carly." She started to cry again.

Carly reached for Liv's hand, just now noticing the IV line. She wanted to say something to comfort her baby sister, but her face was numb, so she took her sister's hand and closed her eyes.

She must have nodded off, the medicine making things soupy. She woke in a different room. Dana Scully sobbed as she clung to Fox Mulder on a television mounted high on the wall. Her mother was sleeping in a pink recliner. Liv sat at Carly's bedside. Assessing her new surroundings made the room spin. She shut her eyes and waited for the motion to stop. When she dared open them, Liv was standing at the side of the bed, leaning in, almost touching Carly's battered face.

"You're awake. How do you feel? Do you need anything? Some water, juice? The nurse showed me where they keep the ice cream. She said I could get you some when you woke up."

Carly slowly shook her head. She wasn't hungry and the thought of attempting to eat, even ice cream, made her face throb. Liv's shoulders slumped.

"Mother called Janace. She said Father couldn't come up tonight. Chip has some football thing that won't be done until visiting hours are over. Nurse Patsy said I could stay here with you. We went home while you were asleep and packed some things. This was under the welcome mat." Liv held up a piece of yellow construction paper. The handwritten words Get Well Soon! crowned a drawing of a stick-figure woman, child, and small dog. It was signed, "Your neighbors, Sally, Brice and Roscoe."

She fought to keep her eyes open but was losing the battle. As she drifted off, Liv said, "Love you a million." She wasn't sure if she muttered a reply as her mind fuzzily drifted to their father. She wondered if he would feel bad when she saw him next, or if he would make fun of her face and clunky braces.

The next afternoon, while a nurse went over Carly's home

care instructions with Mother, Carly watched Liv palm the bottle of painkillers the nurse set on the table next to her hospital bed. Liv effortlessly opened the childproof bottle and shook several of the pills into her hand. Next, the girl wrapped the pills in tissue and carefully put them in her sweater pocket. Liv saw her older sister eyeing her as she completed her mission and lifted a finger to her pursed lips as she placed the bottle back on the table.

Mother would keep the strong stuff for herself and find some substitute from the medicine cabinet at home that wouldn't be enough to quiet Carly's pain. The girls learned this harsh truth when Liv woke the night she broke her arm. Through clenched teeth and tears, Liv cried, "It hurts so bad, like burning, and itching, and buzzy." Carly took it upon herself to get Liv's pain medication from the kitchen counter. When she tapped the bottle, she recognized the pill that fell into her hand. It wasn't the blue pill Liv had taken earlier. It was the baby aspirin Mother gave them for fevers.

Carly didn't tell Liv at the time, instead bringing her an extra one of the pink chewables with a glass of water. She told her little sister to swallow the pills whole and held her until she cried herself to sleep. The fear she had given her sister too much medicine terrified her and kept her awake for the rest of the night. She sat on the edge of Liv's bed, watching and listening to her sister's breathing to make certain nothing went wrong.

Chapter Five

2022

By the time Carly let the distant memory fade from her mind, brooding clouds had gathered strength. Angry wind and rolling skies settled upon Stillwater, darkening the day, warning of rain. Carly felt like she was sleepwalking as she parked her car at the Roadside Motel, noting only one other vehicle in the grungy parking lot. Inside, she had to laugh, as nothing had changed in the old motel. Dark wood paneling and tired orange tile shrunk the lobby. The furniture was certainly older than her and behind the desk, actual keys hung on small hooks; a faded diamond-shaped fob dangled from each.

In the office behind the desk, a television blared; a meteorologist detailed the escalating storm with unjustified urgency. She tapped the old-fashioned bell, noting its off-key clang was barely audible. From the office, a voice yelled, "Coming!"

A girl, certainly still in high school, bounced out of the office.

"Wow, you're the first human I've laid eyes on today," the girl announced.

"Kind of dead, huh?" Carly replied.

"It's hard for the Roadside to compete with all the new hotels popping up on this side of town. I'm hoping you need a room?"

"Yes, I do. Uncle Mark, uh, well, he's not really my uncle. I've just called him that all my life. He's my dad's best friend, but you didn't ask about that, sorry." Carly took a breath to compose herself. Exhaustion was quickly turning her mind to mush. "Mr. Watts said he'd save the best room for me," Carly said, digging through her purse for her debit card.

"You must be Carly. He told me you'd be in. I'm Iva. Hate to say I'm not sure which one is the best or the worst, but most people seem to prefer the unit on the end. You only share a wall with one neighbor that way, but the way things are going, you can take your pick."

"Sure, the one on the end would be great."

Carly handed her card to the young girl, but she refused.

"Mr. Watts said this was on the house."

"Really? That was nice of him. I usually stay with my sister, but she has a new baby. Her house is a little over-crowded these days."

Iva handed the key to Carly.

"Um, if you need clean towels or anything, just ring," the girl said, picking up the phone, putting it to her ear for a moment before setting it back on the hook. "Had to make sure this old thing is still working. Vending machines and ice are in the breezeway. I'm kind of new here. I can't think of anything else."

"No worries. I've been driving for the past sixteen hours. I just need a clean place to crash out for a while. Oh, and a hot shower."

"I think that room has you covered, then. Enjoy your stay."

Carly nodded to the girl and walked to her car. The room was a short distance from where she parked, but she got in her car and reparked in the spot in front of the door to her room. She wasn't sure she was inside the lines of the space as the paint was too faded and chipped. It looked as if she were the only occupant, so she wasn't too concerned.

The key needed a bit of finessing before she heard a click and the door swung open. She flipped the light switch and shook the rain out of her hair. Taking the room in, she was impressed to see that Uncle Mark had sprung for new bedding at some point in the past ten years. Playing to his audience, he'd chosen a bright orange bedspread with black and white accents, the colors of the state college that was the life force of Stillwater. There was only a hint of mustiness, but the room was stuffy, the air stale. She went to the air conditioner and turned it on, cranking the cold air down to frigid, the way she liked it.

She grabbed her toiletry bag and a fresh T-shirt and sweatpants out of her suitcase and headed for the bathroom, which she was pleasantly surprised to find had received a complete makeover. As was a ritual with her, she lined up her hair products, makeup, and hygiene items on the counter as she brushed her teeth. A shower sounded good, but she was so tired, sleep won. She used the restroom and changed into clean clothes.

Satisfied that the room had cooled to near arctic temperatures, she turned the lights off, chose the bed closest to the bathroom and farthest from the door, and crawled under the blankets. She plugged in her phone charger and set an alarm for four hours. Liv dropped numerous texts indicating how badly she wanted to see her. As she rested her head on the pillow, her phone pinged again. She reached for it and pulled it to her without lifting her head.

LIV: *OK, I know you are in Stillwater now. I stalked Life360. Guess you are safe and need some sleep. Call me as soon as you wake up. Can't wait to see you! Love you a million.*

"A billion million," Carly muttered to the empty room.

She put the phone back on the table, then doubting Liv would allow her to sleep until the alarm woke her, snatched it back up and silenced notifications.

The mattress was lumpy, but it felt good to lie down, and she was asleep in seconds. The sounds of rolling thunder and heavy rainfall serenaded her as she slept.

Carly jolted awake and shot upright in the bed. The television was on, the volume ear-shattering. She groped the bedside table for the remote. It was held on the table with Velcro. Was this some lamebrain attempt to deter theft? She didn't know. All she did know was that the television had switched itself on, and it was so loud it shook the windows. She ripped the remote from the table and fumbled for the volume button. Punching the volume down button did no good. *Great, the battery is dead,* she thought. On screen, two cars revved their engines and took off down what looked to be Hollywood Boulevard. The sound made her head hurt and the room spin. She grappled with the remote again, this time locating the *power* button, which, of course, wouldn't work either if the batteries were dead.

She shook the twisted sheets off of her and almost face-planted when one foot got caught in the bedspread as she dashed to the television. She attempted to kill the power, but the television blared on. The volume was louder, and she was certain the decibels were climbing as she leaned over the back of the dresser, grasping desperately for the power cord. A groan escaped her mouth. The cord was held firmly in the wall and secured by a barred cage. No matter how hard she tried to yank the plug free, it didn't give.

Her fuzzy mind could not think of any other way to quiet the screaming television. She scanned the room, her eyes first landing on the ice bucket. For a moment she considered filling it with water and dousing the TV to death, but rationality grabbed her and she didn't fight back. Next, she reached for the comforter on the extra bed, yanked it off, and threw it over the TV like one would choke out a fire. Still, the speaker wailed even louder.

She grabbed her phone, yanking it free of the charger and ran to the bathroom, slamming the thin door behind her. It offered little defense to the resounding assault of the television speakers. Unlocking her phone, she scrolled through her contacts, searching for Uncle Mark's information. She had the phone number for the Roadside saved under his name. Just as she settled her finger over the call icon, the room fell silent. Her eyes darted around the small bathroom and her body tensed, awaiting another raucous reanimation of the television. She froze in place for several minutes, noting the sun now sneaking through the small, opaque window high on the bathroom wall. The rushing sounds from nearby Highway 51 whispered through the walls. The storm had passed while she slept.

Gathering courage, she opened the bathroom door, her phone held in front of her like a weapon. She had slept for only three hours before the television woke her. She scanned the room, searching for any sign of an intruder, when a text notification buzzed on her phone. Startled by the noise, she dropped it and a yelp escaped her lips. *But I silenced notifications,* she thought as she picked the phone up and drew it to her face. The icons on the screen confirmed she had quieted her phone so she could sleep uninterrupted—a couple of missed calls, several texts, Facebook and Instagram notices.

She nearly dropped the phone again when she saw the most recent notification had come from her father's phone. A simple text...

FATHER: *Welcome home, Carly. I've missed my firstborn.*

This time Carly threw the phone onto the bed like she'd picked up something too hot to touch. A text message from her deceased father was the last thing she'd expected. She eyed the phone suspiciously, waiting for another sign the electronics in the room were possessed.

Hesitantly, she approached the television and peeked under the comforter before yanking it off and hurling it back to the bed. She studied the flat screen, on-edge and bracing herself. The television remained silent as she took the few steps back to the nightstand. She retrieved the remote and pushed the *power* button while another finger hovered over the volume down button, prepared. To her surprise, the volume was at a normal level and hokey Muzak warbled as images of Stillwater's tourist offerings scrolled on-screen: The National Wrestling Museum, botanic gardens, two of the town's most notorious restaurants and a few other highlights. She had to laugh to herself as the Roadside Motel was more popular with frat house keggers, illicit liaisons, and after-hour get-togethers than with tourists. The only time the *No Vacancy* sign ever blinked was during rival football battles and graduation season, when the town's newer lodging options were filled to capacity. The images and music were decidedly vintage; the vibe was in desperate need of a refresh.

Her phone rang, frightening her again, and she dropped the remote. It was Liv. There would be no more napping until after dinner. Which was fine. She was too spooked to get any more sleep and wanted only to escape the confines of the room as quickly as possible.

"Hey Liv, I'll be over soon—"

"It's me, Aunt Carly! Not Mommy!"

"Me who?" she asked, stifling a giggle.

"Fallon! Silly!" the little girl replied. Her niece hadn't mastered her own name yet and pronounced it "Fow-win."

"This can't be Fallon. Whoever this is sounds too grown up!"

"Mommy, you take it. Aunt Carly doesn't know who I am." The child's voice faded as she took the phone to her mother, defeated. Carly felt bad for confusing the poor girl.

"Carly?"

"Yes, sister. It's your sister. I think I made Fallon mad. Sorry!"

"No worries. Her moods turn on a dime these days. So, hey, Derek's fixing to throw some steaks on the grill and I'm dying to hug your neck ... so, get on over here!"

"Yum! Okay, let me freshen up. I still have a bit of road buzz. I'm sure a home-cooked meal and a glass of wine will take the edge off." She considered her need for a shower and decided it could wait in light of the text message and TV issues. "I'll be over as quick as I can. Need me to grab anything on my way?"

"Nope, just need you. Hurry up!"

The call ended and Carly quickly got ready. She rummaged through her suitcase and changed, wrapping a hoodie around her waist. Early Oklahoma springtime could be fickle. Once the sun set, it was bound to be chilly. She grabbed her phone and threw it in her purse, then snatched up the room key from the dresser. As she made her way to the door, a thought occurred to her, and she turned back. In the bathroom she turned on the light, then moved to the table that sat between the two beds and turned the lamp on. Finally at the door, she switched the main light on for the room as well. Coming back to an empty motel room was always a bit frightening, but returning to this room alone in the dark was too scary to imagine.

Outside, the remnants of the early May storm lay strewn about the parking lot, catkins, cherry blossom petals, and cottonwood fluff scattered about like nature's confetti. The air smelled clean, and the storm washed away a layer of the red dirt that clung to everything in Stillwater.

Driving through town evoked a deluge of memories, some despised while others enjoyed. Every corner held a reminder of the years from her childhood until the time she left Still-water to escape her hometown. She drove the haunted streets with three windows down. The car stereo remained silent. The only noise was the rush of the wind through the windows and the residual ghostly echoes summoned by her tired mind. Recollections jumped from here to there as she strayed from the course to her sister's house and found herself sitting outside of the church at 7th Street and Duck.

Chapter Six

1996

Carly watched the jubilant wedding party erupt from the church doors. They sat in an empty parking lot on Duck Street in the backseat of Mother's Crown Victoria. Arriving before the nuptials were scheduled to begin, Mother chain-smoked and watched the guests pour into the chapel, many of them her former clients and friends. Minutes before the bride and groom burst out of the ornate doors, she took two pills from her purse and washed them down with a Bartles and Jaymes. She raised the bottle to her ex as he held his new bride and posed for pictures. Her eyes were fixed on the woman in the white gown.

"Take a good look, girls," Mother said. "That's what loving a man'll do for you. One little bump in the road and they bolt. Only Mitch Bennett could fill my shoes this quickly."

Carly tried to keep her younger sister preoccupied by allowing Liv to play with Carly's Barbie. This was a special treat for the young girl, one which Carly rarely allowed. When

Liv got her hands on the doll, she'd mess up her long blond hair and pull her arms off.

Carly pushed herself up in her seat and peered out the car window to see a photographer trailing after Father as he whisked his bride to the awaiting car adorned with streamers and balloons, cans tied to the bumper, its windows exclaiming "Just Married" in white shoe polish. Carly and Liv weren't invited to the wedding.

"Most garish dress I've ever seen," Mother said under her breath.

Carly folded her knees under her so she could get a better look at the dress. She didn't know what garish meant. To Carly, Janace looked like a princess.

"Of all the ironies," Mother spoke, her speech lazy. "This is where your father and I wed." She pointed to the building to the right of the parking lot.

"Good old Payne County Courthouse, shotgun wedding, Justice of the Peace, yada, yada." Mother fell silent as she watched the limousine crawl past the crowd gathered on the sidewalk across the street. "I wore a borrowed dress, and your father made a corsage out of wildflowers. Actually, there were more weeds than flowers, but the sentiment was, well..." Her voice trailed off.

Mother rummaged in the front seat and pulled out another wine cooler.

"You know they used to date, right? Your father dumped Janace when he met me. Bet that galled her to no end, the trollop. I can just see her scanning the newspaper every day, waiting for the divorce listing. Pounced fast and dug her fake red claws into him." Mother smashed another cigarette out in the car's ashtray and immediately lit up another.

The bump in the road she spoke of was more than a bump. Catherine Bennett lost her ability to walk for a time. Mother was an artist whose murals graced the walls of many of Stillwater's finest homes. While painting the last leaf of a forest scene in a fancy new fairy-tale house on the outskirts of town, she reached too far and fell in a stir of frenzied energy and drywall dust as she landed just-so on the concrete floor. She nearly broke her back. The fall caused the small family's lives to spin out of control.

From that point on, Carly never sang the familiar sidewalk song again, having seen the consequences of the careless rhyme, and she always took care not to step on a crack. Doctors agreed that Mother's injury would cause her untold discomfort for an unknown amount of time. After weeks in the hospital, she was released. Carly and Liv, too young to be allowed on her ward, hadn't seen Mother the whole time. She came home in a body cast, white plaster wrapped stiffly from shoulder to knee. It made Mother look like a mummy.

Mitch wasn't equipped to care for an ailing wife, a rowdy toddler, and an infant. Janace swooped in from a reception desk where she worked at one of his businesses and quickly went about unburdening the man. He paid no heed to his soon to be ex-wife during her recovery. As soon as the body cast came off, Mitch moved Catherine and his daughters into the rented duplex that he furnished with the items Janace discarded from the home the four once lived in. By the time the lease was up, Mother was so mired in her own misery she didn't bother seeking a more suitable home. She re-upped the contract and there they stayed.

Mother's descent into addiction didn't happen overnight. There were times she tried to pull herself up and make a new life for her two daughters. Carly remembered more than Liv. While it was confusing and difficult adjusting to life without their father in their cramped duplex, there were moments of happiness. Carly's fondest memories were of her mother getting her ready for school. Each morning, Mother would wake Carly and describe an album cover from her collection. The turntable and records had belonged to their grandmother.

Catherine Bennett clung to the past by clinging to the songs she grew up with, and passed on her love of tunes from days gone by to her daughters. Carly felt grown up as she carefully lowered the needle down to the LP, making sure to never scratch the black disk. "Let's listen to the one with the pregnant lady in the white dress on the cover," her mother would tell her. Carly would diligently flip through her mother's albums until she found Carly Simon (her namesake) smiling on the front of *Hotcakes*. Carly's favorite was Elton John's *Captain Fantastic and the Brown Dirt Cowboy*, even though the record cover kind of scared her. Her mother would sing along as she toasted waffles or Pop-Tarts, or scrambled eggs. Carly still knew every word of those songs by heart.

Over time, their mother lost her grip on life. There was no music in the house anymore. There was no laughter. On the girls' best days, there would still be waffles or Pop-Tarts, but Carly did the toasting, worried Liv might burn herself or the food if left alone to the task. On other days, there was no food. She would knock on her mother's bedroom door and ask when she was going to the grocery store. There was no telling how or if her mother would react.

When their school started serving breakfast, Carly brought the paperwork to her mother.

"If you fill this out, we can eat breakfast at school. It's free."

It took her mother over a week to get around to filling out the forms. But once she had, Carly and Liv didn't start their school days with empty stomachs.

———

Carly pulled away from the church, her mind still swimming with the images of her father on his wedding day; an event she wished she'd never witnessed, the words of "Haven't Got Time for the Pain" whispering in her mind.

Chapter Seven

2022

Fallon waved enthusiastically from the front window of the house as Carly pulled into her sister's driveway. Carly rolled up the windows and went to the porch. Before she could knock, Fallon flung the door open and rushed out, throwing her arms around Carly's legs.

"Daddy, she's here! Aunt Carly is here!" the child screamed, abandoning Carly on the stoop and running to find her parents.

Carly didn't wait for an invitation. She stepped inside, shut the door and kicked off her sneakers. The aroma from the grill reached her nose and her mouth watered. She'd eaten nothing but beef jerky and Sour Skittles in the past twenty-four hours. A blue dog with an Australian accent danced on the television in the empty living room.

Liv rushed into the room holding the baby out.

"Quick, take him. He just dropped a bomb in his diaper and I'm going to burn the potatoes!"

Carly took the boy who cooed happily, unperturbed by his own foul scent. This was the first time she'd held her new nephew, and he was almost six months old. She'd seen him during their weekly FaceTime get-togethers, but it didn't compare to holding him.

She made her way down the hall in search of the nursery. Her brother-in-law, Derek, almost ran into her as he left his own bedroom.

"Oh, hey, Carly! It's good to see you! Had a call from the hospital. These days I have to hide in the bathroom to take work calls. Oh wow, hate to be rude, but you stink!" he said, fanning his face with his hand.

"Very funny. It's your son. His room is on the right, right?"

"Yes. Sure you don't want me to take him?"

"No, I've got this. Little Asa sure knows how to make a memorable first impression, doesn't he?" She spoke baby talk and Asa slobbered on her arm as she entered the nursery. A mural depicting an underwater seascape was artfully painted on one wall. Liv had their mother's talent.

After changing Asa, she joined the rest of the family in the kitchen. Liv grabbed the baby from Carly and wrestled him into a high chair.

"You're just in time. Fallon, tell Aunt Carly what night it is?"

"It's Taco Tuesday! My favorite!"

"I thought your favorite was Pizza Wednesday," Derek replied.

"That's my favorite, too."

"I've never said no to a taco, but I was promised steak," Carly said.

"And steak you will have," Liv replied. "Anything can become a taco when you put it in a taco shell. Even steak." She gave a double wink to her sister.

After dinner, Derek wrangled Fallon into the bathroom as the child loudly protested. Carly held Asa, who wiggled and rooted impatiently. Liv handed a baby bottle to Carly and set a wineglass on the table next to her. She lifted her own glass in a toast.

"Here's to the wonders of the breast pump! First glass of wine in sixteen months," she said before plopping down in the recliner across from Carly. "So, how are you doing with all this?"

"You mean Father dying?"

"Well, yeah, that was at the top of the list."

"I don't know. I mean, I guess it really hasn't had that great an impact on me, well, aside from my bank account. Gas is stupid expensive. Let's be honest, Mitch Bennett crosses my mind about as often as I crossed his."

"Time to burp him," Liv whispered. "I guess I get that. Maybe it's different for me because I live here still, but I'm kind of sad. Sad that my kids won't know him."

"Sorry, Liv, how much has he seen your kids since they were born? By the way, what was the cause of his death? I mean, you said he was home when he died. What happened? Heart attack? Accident? I'm sort of disturbed that this question has just now come to me," Carly said as she gently bounced Asa, his head on her shoulder while she rubbed circles on his back with her palm. After a few minutes, the infant burped loudly in her ear, and she cradled him again as he eagerly reached for the bottle and worked on draining its contents.

"Well, the unofficial story is the virus."

"The virus? The fake news, five-G plandemic virus?"

"Yes, that one. They've been deniers since day one, so I'm not sure how this narrative will play out. He'd been sick, bedridden. Janace wanted to attend a rally—don't ask—in Tulsa, and asked Rachel to come sit with him. Little known fact ... Rachel used to be a nurse assistant."

"So Rachel found him? Ugh, that's horrible. It's got to be bad enough being married to Chip, but to take care of an ailing Mitch only to find him dead…" Carly grimaced and threw in a fake shudder for effect.

"Yeah, there are conflicting stories, especially when asked how her husband died of a disease she believed to be nonexistent. But I don't know, he's dead. I get all my intel from Uncle Mark. He says Janace has pushed to list the cause of death as complications related to the virus, and she wants him cremated as quickly as possible."

"Cremated?" Carly exclaimed, only to realize Asa was asleep in her arms. "Cremated?" she asked again, whispering. "Didn't he shell out a ton of money on a custom mausoleum for four? Why would he want to be cremated?"

"You don't need to whisper. He'd sleep through a hurricane. Just another mystery surrounding the whole thing. Janace insists he changed his mind recently, wanted to be cremated. Who knows? Rumor has it he may have amended his will, but he never mentioned how he wanted his remains dealt with, so she has carte blanche to light him up. Sorry, that was tacky. This wine is going straight to my hardened heart." Liv raised her glass again. "You better get on that, or I'll drink yours, too."

Carly grabbed her glass and brought it to her lips. She'd finally found what she needed to shake the anxiety tying her in knots the past few days.

"I think those rumors of a will change are legit," Liv said.

"Really?"

"And this didn't just come from Uncle Mark. Good thing you are sitting—Father called me…" Liv let the words hang in the air, pressing down on them like a weight while she swirled her glass and took another sip.

"Called you?" Carly questioned. "Like, picked up the phone and dialed your number?"

"Yep! Just like that. Talk about a shock. I can't remember when he called me last. I was sure someone had died. But get this, you won't believe why he called…" Liv paused and took a drink from her glass, emptying it in one large gulp. Derek entered the room, the front of his T-shirt wet.

"It wasn't easy, but she is clean and she's asleep," he commented.

Liv held the empty wineglass over her head.

"Bartender, pour me another."

"One more. You should watch yourself. Ease back in maybe," he said with a smile on his face.

"Cut me some slack. I've been dry for so long and I pumped enough milk to get him through until this time tomorrow. Momma's earned this." Her speech was slurred, each word sliding off her tongue loosely.

"I can't stand the suspense. What did Mitch want when he called you?"

"Oh man, Carly, I'm kind of afraid to tell you..."

"Stop it! Tell me!"

Derek came back into the room and poured Liv another glass. Before he sat and filled his, he tried to top Carly's off. She blocked it with her hand.

"Gotta drive back to the Roadside," she whispered. "Liv, come on."

"Okay, okay. Said he was rewriting his will and wanted to know how much I thought was fair for him to leave to us." Liv leaned forward, her eyes grew wide and she pointed at Carly, lifting a finger off her wine glass to do so. Then she slumped back in her chair and took another drink.

"How much to leave us? As in you and me?"

"Yep. He went on to say that he'd always done his best to treat all of his kids equally his whole life and wanted to do so in death."

Carly choked on her wine. A bit dribbled down her chin, and she caught it with her finger before it landed on the sleeping infant's head.

"Wait ... he didn't really say that! He treated us all the same?" Carly turned her head, craning her neck in each direction as if looking for something. "Last time I checked, I didn't have a two-acre lot in Camelot Crossing gifted to me. Nor have I gone on safari in Africa, skiing in the Alps, swimming with dolphins in the Bahamas..."

"To be fair, he did gift you a car when you turned sixteen."

"Ah, yes. A Plymouth Fury that was almost as old as him," Carly replied.

"I think that makes it a classic," Derek interjected.

"Right, a classic. It was a boat! I mean, it sat twelve ... comfortably. No lie. Every other time I drove it, the starter had to be replaced. It was a nightmare. It sat on one of his used car lots too long. I'm sure he just did it for the tax write-off. That's how the great Mitch Bennett operates. Operated."

Liv interrupted. "This chick didn't get a car. Not even a beater that broke down frequently. Meanwhile, on their sixteenth birthdays, the prince and princess of Bennett Manor were gifted the car of their choosing from one of the more upscale car lots Mitch owned. And while we're making comparisons, let's talk about our equal weddings, shall we?"

"Uh-oh, now you stepped in it, Carls. We're going down the wedding lane. Hold on," Derek said.

"Hush, Derek! This 'equal treatment' pipe dream blows up when it comes to weddings." Liv flashed finger quotes, her face turning red. The pain of the memory sank into her eyes. "He sent a blender from our registry and didn't show up. I guess Janace couldn't risk being seen at a backyard ceremony. He didn't offer a dime to help. We'd have barely scraped enough for an at-home garden ceremony if it weren't for Derek's parents."

Liv brushed away the tears that inched down her face. They should have known better than to talk about their parents while they drank.

"On the bright side, now that my residency is complete, we are saving up for a dream honeymoon," Derek chimed in.

Liv nodded her head, and a smile flashed on her face when she gazed at him.

"You're lucky you didn't come home for Kimmi's wedding. No expense was spared. She arrived in a horse-drawn carriage. Who does that?" Liv shook her head before lifting her wineglass to her mouth.

"Okay, aside from the blatant delusions the man believed about himself and his parenting skills, I have to say, I never thought my name would grace the pages of his will. What'd you tell him?"

"I was stumped. I mean, really, how do you answer a question like that?"

"I told her to say it was easy. With four kids, simple math would be to quarter it," Derek replied.

"Did you say that to him?" Now Carly was the animated one, leaning into the question, her lips pulled into an "O" shape.

"Of course not. You know I can't stand up to that man. He tried to go there again at Chip's campaign rally. Brought the whole pretext up again ... in a speech to half the town! What the—"

"I can vouch for her. It was classic Mitch Bennett. And Janace played along."

"Yes, she did! He had the audacity to espouse his belief that he had raised his four kids well. And Janace sat there nodding her head!"

Carly knew the story well, but that didn't prevent her from spitting out a few drops of wine as she gasped. The ruby liquid landed on her nephew's pudgy cheek. A wave of guilt washed over her, and she quickly wiped it away with her sleeve.

"I swear I thought I was being punked. I kept looking around, waiting for a camera crew to rush in. Treated us all equally? Raised us well? I mean, I can't even imagine a world where he thought any of that was true. And Janace, ugh, Janace sitting there nodding her head as if she agreed with it all. The woman who always found an excuse as to why we shouldn't sleep over during visitation weekends, the nerve."

"Delusional, both of them," Derek said. "We all know that the man who raised the two of you is a completely different person from the man who raised Chip and Kimmi."

The conversation lulled. Carly's mind went to the many times the girls were floored by the excesses in their half-siblings' lives. She wondered if Liv nodded off; she was so still, but she shifted in her seat and took a large swig of wine.

"So, how about this Chip for City Council weirdness?" Derek spoke, filling the silence. "I don't know about you two, but I'd have a hard time voting for a grown man who has never sat down for a job interview in his entire life. Talk about riding on his dad's coattails."

"Not getting my vote," Liv said. She tried to take a drink, but her shoulders slumped as she realized her glass was empty. Despite Liv's animated retelling of the story, her eyes grew droopy and the hand that held the wine glass drooped as well. Carly took the last swig of her wine and turned to Derek.

"You want to take him? I should head back to the motel."

"No, Carly, stay," Liv whined.

"I'm almost as tired as you are, Liv."

"Oh, all right. Just leave me." Liv stood and swayed as she walked to Carly. After Derek took Asa, Liv wrapped her arms around her sister and squeezed tightly. Carly wasn't sure if Liv really wanted a hug or just wanted someone to prop her up. She kissed Liv on the forehead.

"We'll see each other tomorrow. What time is our rendezvous at Bennett Manor?" Carly asked, making her way toward the door. Liv leaned on her heavily.

"Not until two o'clock. I'll pick you up. Oooh, let's do breakfast ... Just Wafflin'? Sounds so good." Liv opened the door and they walked onto the front porch.

"I don't know, Liv. I really need to sleep. I don't want to wake up early."

"Sleep? What is this sleep you speak of? Derek, have you any idea what she is talking about?" Liv turned to her husband and Carly took the opportunity to shift her sister's weight onto Derek. Liv slumped further in the arms of her husband and batted at a stray hair.

"I vaguely remember it from my youth," Derek replied. His statement was punctuated with a loud yawn.

"You two chose to procreate, so I have no guilt."

"Well, I'll be up before the sun, so if you can't sleep, let me know. Otherwise, I'll meet you at the house at two o'clock."

"Sounds good! Good night, you two!"

"Carly!" Liv's voice broke as she grabbed her sister's wrist. "You know what this means now, don't you?"

"It means that we may or may not eat waffles tomorrow..."

"No, not that. What this means to us. What we are now..." A tear slid down Liv's face.

"Not sure I follow, Liv. Go back inside, get some sleep."

"It means we're orphans now." Liv choked the words out and grabbed Carly's hand before crumbling into her husband, her body shaking with heaving sobs.

"Hey, hey, stop that," Carly said, turning to her sister. "We're grown women, not orphans."

"Getting this one to bed before things get even sloppier," Derek said, gently guiding Liv toward the house.

Liv and Derek waved Carly off from their front porch. Liv called out, "Love you a million!"

"Million, billion," Carly yelled.

When the sun fell, the temperature dropped at least twenty degrees. Carly pulled her hoodie on before getting in the car.

She gave up on music before she'd exited Liv's neighborhood. Each song abruptly ended when the car stereo shut off, leaving her singing solo. Must be a loose wire, she told herself.

She resorted to scanning channels and settled on local sports. An announcer calling the OSU Cowgirls' softball game pushed out the quiet. She knew nothing about the sport but couldn't stand to drive in silence. The loose wire didn't interrupt the game.

Despite the announcer's best efforts, she was unable to keep her mind from wandering back to the day they lost Mother. Something changed in her that day. It was as if she ran out of tears; she could muster none for the woman who raised her. The years of addiction, apathy, and neglect had long before tipped the scales. Mother's demons and Father's desertion tarnished the good years. Carly disagreed with her sister. They weren't recently left without parents; they'd been orphaned long ago.

Chapter Eight

2016

Carly pulled into the driveway of the duplex just before eleven o'clock the night before the graduation ceremony. She'd told her sister not to wait up, but as she gathered her purse and duffle bag, lights flooded the driveway. Liv bounded out the front door and raced to her sister, grabbing Carly around the waist, shaking her back and forth.

"You're here! You made it! I'm so happy!"

Somewhere nearby a dog barked, and a porch light came on across the street.

"Be quiet! Mrs. Stinson is going to call the cops on us!" Carly said, trying to whisper, but laughing too hard to be quiet.

"The Bennett girls, disturbing the peace again," Liv replied.

"Of course, I'm here. Like I'd miss my baby sister graduating from college!" she said, shoving her duffle bag into Liv's arms before grabbing some fast-food trash and an empty coffee cup. She shut her car door and threw an arm around her sister's neck, and they made their way to the decaying duplex.

Inside, Carly threw her road trip litter in the kitchen garbage can and found a couple of beers in the refrigerator while Liv took her bag to the room the two had shared for so many years.

"Mother didn't wait up for me?" Carly said, as she entered the bedroom and handed her sister a beer. She made no effort to conceal her sarcasm.

"Um, nah, she's been passed out for an hour or two. Gotta get her beauty sleep. Tomorrow's a big day."

Carly rolled her eyes. "But of course."

Liv's cap and gown hung outside the closet door.

"Put it on! Fashion show! Fashion show!" Carly urged.

"It's one lame getup, Carly. It doesn't qualify as a fashion show. Besides, you've seen one cap and gown, you've seen them all."

"I don't think so," Carly said, grabbing the gown and removing the sheer garment bag. "You worked hard for this! This," Carly continued as she unzipped the gown and grabbed Liv's hand, dragging her off the bed. "This is the best cap and gown ever! It represents two jobs, a full credit load—"

"Don't forget a mountain of debt," Liv chimed in, reluctantly allowing her sister to drag her from the bed and sliding her arms into the sleeves of the gown.

"We'll just forget about that mountain of debt for the time being," Carly said as she nudged her sister toward the full-length mirror. It was still adorned with stickers ranging from My Little Pony to boy bands to political statements documenting their transition from little girls to young women.

"I'm hopeful there's a future doctor in my life to help me pay that debt off," Liv said, her cheeks flushed.

Carly had been standing behind her sister admiring how fitting the gown looked on her, and now spun Liv around by her shoulders.

"A doctor? This Derek guy, huh? You thinking he's the one?"

"Yes, yes, I am thinking that!"

"Wow! Your life is full of excitement these days!"

"What about your life? Any new guys? How's the job?" Liv removed the gown, zipped it up, and carefully pulled the cover over it before returning it to the hook on the closet door.

"Hmmm, my life in Tempe ... it's fine, I guess. Still writing jingles and copy for used car salesmen; slightly hopeful I might bust out of the entry level copywriter status sometime in the next ten to fifteen years. As for my love life, it's just Clovis sharing my bed with me. No prospects on the horizon."

"Sounds like someone needs to try harder," Liv said before stifling a yawn.

"Thank you for that astute advice."

"Anytime! I'm a college graduate now. I do what I can."

"Time for bed," Carly said with a laugh, whacking her sister in the head with a pillow. "I'm beat."

They went to the small bathroom together and brushed their teeth, both huddled over the single sink that bore countless char marks from dropped curling irons and colored globs of spilled nail polish before climbing into their respective beds. The two continued to whisper and giggle in the dark until Carly heard her sister's breathing deepen. Quietly, she said, "Love you a million," before she fell asleep.

Carly woke up far earlier than she preferred. She always had a hard time sleeping on the first night back, and the old twin bed was well past its prime. She crept quietly from the room, freshened up, and headed out to her car. Her cell phone sat dead in the console. She'd forgotten to bring it into the house and made a mental note to charge it when she returned. The sun was just rising, the old neighborhood still sleeping. She wanted to get some things to mark the occasion and drove to the grocery store that was now open twenty-four hours.

Such things were commonplace in Tempe, but still somewhat novel to Stillwater.

She was pleased to see the town didn't yet have a need for an all-night grocery store, as the parking lot was practically empty. The greeting cards in the graduation section were picked over, but she found one she liked. Next, she grabbed some Mylar balloons and a bouquet before going to the bakery department. She chose a cake decorated in black and orange icing, adorned with a plastic graduation cap, and asked the bakery attendant to add "Liv" under Congratulations.

As Carly turned into the neighborhood, she saw flashing lights between the houses. *Bet Mrs. Stinson took another fall,* she thought. But as she got nearer, her heart sank and her legs shook. The ambulance was sitting in front of her childhood house. "No, no, no, no," she repeated aloud, scanning the scene in a desperate effort to figure out what was going on. Her legs weren't functioning properly, the shaking making it impossible to drive any further. She slammed on the brake and threw the gear into park, leaving the car in the middle of the street. Her beat-up Civic was barely at a complete stop before she was out and running. As she neared the house, the front door opened, and an EMT exited, easing a gurney over the threshold. She couldn't see who was on the stretcher.

"Liv!" she screamed as she pushed through a group of neighbors clustered at the end of the driveway, some still in their robes.

Her sister exited the house behind a second paramedic, her arms wrapped around herself, her face red, her expression confused. She looked so small, so vulnerable. Carly's heart took another dive inside her chest. Nothing made sense. *I should have left a note for her. Why didn't I leave a note?*

"Liv!" she screamed again.

Carly ran past the EMT, barely glancing at her mother laid out on the stretcher, looking as if she was asleep.

Reaching Liv, she grabbed her arms. "Liv, what's going on? What's wrong with her?"

"I, I … don't know," Liv stammered, trying to find words. "I went to wake her up, take her a cup of coffee. I wanted her to be—" Her words trailed off as sobs overtook her. "She wouldn't wake up, Carls. I couldn't wake her up. I didn't know what to do. You were gone. I called 9-1-1. They say she's unresponsive. I just, I just didn't know what to do."

"Ma'am, will you be following us to the hospital?" an EMT questioned, climbing into the back of the ambulance.

"Uh, yeah, okay," Carly replied. "Liv, do you want to change?" Liv was still wearing old sweatpants that were too big for her and a Pistol Pete T-shirt.

"No, no. Let's just go. Can you drive? I don't think I can."

"Of course." Carly guided Liv to the car in the middle of the road, the driver's door still open.

The two followed the ambulance in stunned silence. About a mile out from the hospital, Liv asked, "Why haven't they turned the lights and sirens on?"

Carly dropped her sister near the ambulance bay. "I'll park and come find you," she said. Liv nodded as if she'd heard, but Carly wasn't sure if her words registered.

Carly parked and sprinted to the entrance of the ER. She spotted Liv sitting alone, hugging herself, rocking back and forth. Carly went to her, putting her arm around her, pulling her close and rubbing her arm. She was so cold.

"The nurse said they would have someone come talk to us soon," Liv said, her voice sounding dreamy, trance-like.

"Okay, you good? You want me to go get you some coffee? I might have a sweater in the back of my car."

"No, thank you. I should call Derek," Liv replied. "I left my cell phone at home."

"Yeah, yeah, good idea. Ask him to bring a jacket, maybe. You're so cold." Carly took in her surroundings, spotting a courtesy phone on a table nearby. "My phone is dead, but there's a phone over there."

Liv stared at where Carly was pointing, but it took her a while to get up and walk over. She sat in the open seat next to the courtesy phone and then stared at it for a time as well. Just as Carly thought she should go help her sister with the task, Liv lifted the handset and dialed. Carly couldn't hear her sister's end of the conversation, but saw that she was crying again, having to explain the inexplicable to Derek. A few minutes later, she hung up and sat where she was for a bit too long. Slowly she turned her head, seeming to notice her sister for the first time, got up and walked to where Carly sat.

"He's on his way," Liv murmured.

Before Derek arrived, a very young man in a lab coat entered the lobby, pausing to speak to the woman behind the entry desk. The nurse pointed to Carly and Liv. The young man straightened his tie and his lab coat and approached the girls. "Ms. Bennetts?" he said to the two of them.

"Yes, I'm Carly, and this is my sister Liv." Carly spoke for the two of them. His name tag said Dr. Todd Hulas. *Doctor? He's so young.*

"Perhaps we can talk in one of the family rooms." The doctor reached his arm out as if to help Carly up. She didn't take his hand.

"Um, okay." She did offer her hand to Liv. "Let's go, Liv."

The two followed the impossibly youthful Dr. Hulas to a small room. "Have a seat," he said, closing the door and motioning to the small sofa opposite the doorway.

He sat across from them, his back stiff, his demeanor hinting he'd rather be almost anywhere else than here in this tiny space with Carly and Liv.

"We did what we could to help your mother. Unfortunately, she was deprived of oxygen too long, and I am sorry to tell you this, but she has died."

Liv, finally shaken from her reverie, began to sob; great heaving, gasping sobs. Carly sat unmoved.

Dr. Hulas continued, "While an autopsy will need to be performed, there is evidence both at the scene and in your mother's appearance of an overdose and perhaps chronic alcohol usage. Are you aware of your mother having problems with prescription opioids?"

She didn't mean to; she wished she hadn't, but what Carly did next was laugh. Fortunately, Liv didn't seem to notice and Dr. Hulas—well, she figured doctors, even super new doctors who couldn't possibly be old enough to be sitting here asking her if she was aware of her mother's "problem"—even those doctors were probably used to all kinds of reactions upon telling people of the passing of a loved one.

"Um, yeah, we are aware. It's kind of been her thing for a long time." Carly realized she probably sounded like a horrible person.

"I see. Well, I'm very sorry. Here's my card. If you have any questions, you can give my office a call. A nurse will be in shortly. She can take you to see your mother, if you would like. Some people like to have one last visit, to say goodbye and such."

"Thank you, Doctor," Carly said, standing. She didn't know what else she was supposed to say. *Scurry along, we got this. Good day, sir.*

"Again, I'm sorry for your loss," he said before leaving the room.

As soon as the door closed, Carly began pacing the small room like a caged animal. Liv did not look up, didn't seem to notice she wasn't alone in the room. The constant motion wasn't enough to purge Carly of the anger building inside her like a violent storm.

How dare she? She couldn't O.D. on some random day. It had to be on this day, of all days, Liv's big day. She shook her hands and then balled them into fists, all the while telling herself not to punch the wall. She needed to gain control of herself so she could comfort her sister. Her poor, sweet sister. Did Liv remember what day it was? The reason she wasn't going through this alone, but with Carly here? She choked back a scream as it rose from somewhere inside. She hoped Liv would refuse to go see their mother, certain she would pound her fists on her mother's chest and scream in her lifeless face.

A knock at the door forced Carly out of her downward rage spiral. A nurse cracked the door, and leaned in. "Excuse me, ladies, I'm so sorry to interrupt, but there is a gentleman here for Liv Bennett."

Liv looked up in confusion and looked at Carly, her expression hopeless and lost.

"Oh, yes, he's with us. Please have him come in. Thank you," Carly said in a voice that sounded like she was having someone join them at a restaurant, not in the family room at an ER where their dead mother lay somewhere close by.

Derek entered, saw Liv, and rushed to her side. She melted into him. A wave of guilt washed over Carly. She hadn't provided that comfort for her sister, who obviously needed it. She wanted to wrap this up. Get out of here. Go back to the original plan. Graduation, celebration, happiness. Their mother was a seasoned addict. How could she have messed things up right now?

There was another knock on the door, this time the social worker asking if they wanted to see their mother.

"I just don't think I can," Liv said, her tears finally abating. "Is that wrong?"

"Not at all," the social worker assured her. "Everyone reacts differently in these situations. There is no wrong or right."

Well, hallelujah for that, thought Carly. "Yeah, I think I'll pass as well," she said.

Grateful that part was over, and she wouldn't have to take her fury out on her mother's dead body, Carly was able to focus on the next order of business. The social worker talked them through the autopsy process. Liv had one ear pressed into Derek's chest. He held his other hand over her exposed ear as she tried to avoid hearing this part. The social worker asked if they had a funeral home picked out. Liv heard this. The question caused both girls to look at each other. Carly could read her sister's mind. A funeral. How would they pay for that?

Sensing their concern, the social worker continued, "You don't have to make a decision right now. There is time. I'll be giving you some paperwork. There is a number to call with instructions to release the body once the autopsy is complete."

The social worker went over a few more things, grief counseling groups and other bleak bits. Carly sat wondering how someone decided on this line of work. She guessed it wasn't all dealing with confused adult children of dead addicts. There had to be more to it than this; otherwise, how depressing.

The social worker got up to leave. "I know I've given you a lot of information. Everything we've gone over is here in this folder. Nurse Patsy will be in to wrap things up; then you should be free to go. I'm very sorry for your loss."

Those words again. *Your loss.* Carly had a hard time envisioning what the actual loss was. She lost a woman she hadn't spoken to in almost a year, who chose to take too many pills and wash them down with a sip too much vodka last night instead of welcoming her daughter home. The social worker didn't know the part about the oxy-vodka mishap also taking place on the day of her youngest daughter's college graduation. *Sorry for your loss.* Carly gave her a weak smile. She didn't feel the need to say anything. After all, everyone reacted differently to these situations.

As they waited for the nurse, Derek introduced himself to Carly, and the two agreed they wished they were meeting under better circumstances. The three sat in silence for what seemed like an eternity when Carly noticed the time. "Hey, Derek, why don't you run by the house, get Liv's things, and take her to your place to get ready for the ceremony? I'll stay here and deal with all this. I can meet you at the arena."

Liv protested. "Oh, no Carly. I can't go. I'll just skip it. It's just a ceremony, it doesn't matter."

"No!" Carly said with much more force than she intended. Taking a deep breath to calm herself, she knelt in front of her sister and took her hands. "You worked too hard for this. You are walking across that stage. You are wearing that cap and gown. This is happening. I'm not going to let you skip out. It is too important."

"Carls, I'm a wreck. I don't know if I can—"

Carly didn't let her finish. "You can and you will. You will have many more days to mourn. There is only one day to attend your graduation ceremony. It is today, and you are going. Help me out here, Derek?"

"Yeah, babe, I think it is what your mom would want," Derek added.

Nice one, Derek. Completely false, because obviously what she really wanted was to sit in her cramped, dark room in her sad little duplex and get high all by herself. Carly was pleased Derek was following her lead. This guy was good. She liked him.

With a deep sigh, Liv spoke. "Okay, I'll do it. I don't know how I'm going to get through it. I'll probably cry the whole the time, but I'll do it."

"That's the spirit. Go easy on the mascara," Carly said, giving her baby sister a long hug. "Now get out of here. I will see you soon. Love you a million."

"Million billion," Liv replied.

Carly sat alone for at least an hour before another knock came. Nurse Patsy entered. Immediately Carly recognized the nurse and remembered the social worker saying the name. The kind nurse who took care of her all those years ago when she busted her face open, knocking out her giant tooth. Nurse Patsy did not recognize her. Carly wasn't a bloody mess, and sixteen years had etched themselves on her face. The nurse had an inventory of her mother's belongings. There wasn't much: a torn house dress, some underwear, and socks. She had been wearing pearl earrings. The one thing she had kept that their father had given her. Carly was surprised her mother hadn't hocked them by now. There were some documents to sign, and some niceties exchanged. Nurse Patsy was also sorry for Carly's loss. Then they were done.

Returning to her car, she noticed the balloons bobbing merrily in the back seat. She didn't think Liv had even noticed them. The cake had not fared so well. The congratulatory message was a melted blob, settling in an illegible mess on one side where the cake lay askew. Maybe she could fix it, but probably not. Liv would say she couldn't eat, didn't feel like celebrating anyway. She had just enough time to shower and change before the graduation ceremony.

At the duplex, Carly found the spare key still inside the outdoor light fixture as it had been for years. Entering the room where she and her sister had whispered themselves to sleep only hours ago, she was relieved to find Liv's cap and gown gone. Derek succeeded in coaxing Liv along, at least that far. The door to their mother's room was open, which was an odd thing to see, as it was never left open. Carly closed it. She didn't want to deal with any of that right now. She wanted to focus on her sister and her achievement and block the rest out. Her anger threatened to boil over again into bitter tears. She shoved it down.

Carly pushed through the crowds at Gallagher-Iba Arena. She kept her head down so someone from her past wouldn't recognize her. A catch-up conversation would distract her from her mission to find Derek before the ceremony began. She hoped he had been able to get Liv to the ceremony, and she wasn't here alone. She dreaded thinking that she would have to sit with her father and his family. Kicking herself for never charging her phone, she searched the crowd and spotted Derek waving his hands, trying to catch her attention, and made her way up the stadium seating to sit next to him.

"Liv didn't make you save seats for Father and the others, or did you give up the fight?" she asked, noticing there was no space for the others to join them.

"Oh, no. They aren't coming. They are all at some cheerleading thing for Kimmi in Texas this week," he said. "He called earlier to congratulate her. She didn't tell him about your mom. She had just finished doing her makeup and didn't want to ruin it by crying."

Chapter Nine

2022

As Carly turned into the parking lot of the motel, she noticed the place looked deserted. If it weren't for the red neon *Vacancy* sign twitching, one would never believe it was operational. The only other car in the pitted parking lot was the car she assumed Iva drove.

She entered the room that by now was almost too cold, grateful she'd left the lights on. She tossed her purse on the bed and went to the bathroom. There was no doubt she needed to shower. It would have to be a quick one. The vulnerability of being alone and naked crawled over her skin. Before undressing, she grabbed her phone from her purse and set it on the floor just outside the tub. The warm water did nothing to wash away her anxiety.

As she rinsed conditioner out of her hair, she heard her phone alerts. She counted at least four pings, and her thoughts went immediately to Liv. Her poor sister was likely finding it difficult to hop off memory lane, her emotions heightened by lack of sleep and wine.

She wrapped a towel around her hair and another around

her body before stepping out. As she reached for her phone, the television burst to life again, the volume ear-splitting. Leaving her phone behind, she bolted out of the bathroom and fumbled for the remote. It was no use; as before, the buttons on the controller did nothing to quiet the blaring TV. On the screen, girls on roller skates delivered food to old cars while the song "Sixteen Candles" played, setting the scene. This time she immediately grabbed the large blanket and threw it over the television, and instantly it fell silent. She turned in a circle in the room, not really knowing what she was looking for. The swing bar lock on the door was still secured. She pulled the curtain back and pulled on the window with one hand, gripping the towel around herself with the other. The window was locked as well.

Another notification alert dinged on her phone. She went back to the bathroom and snatched it up. Now she hoped it was Liv attempting to contact her. She could use the comfort of another voice right now. A deflated sigh escaped her mouth as she saw the notifications were from Facebook and Insta-gram. Friend requests on social media were no comfort to her. She quickly got dressed and brushed her teeth. Cocooned in a layer of fleece-lined sweats, she felt a little less exposed.

She pocketed her phone and returned to the main room. First, she went to the light switch on the wall by the door, snapping it off. Shadows fell across the room just outside the light of the table lamp next to the bed. She inspected the scene and, deeming it too dark for her comfort, turned the light back on. Typically, she preferred sleeping in pitch black-ness, but tonight she'd make an exception.

She pulled the sheets back on the bed and climbed in, retrieving her phone and swiping it to life. First she clicked on the Facebook notification, but dropped the phone, pushing it away from her as she saw who the request was from: Mitch Bennett, her father, her now deceased father. Trying to settle herself, she took some deep breaths before picking the phone up. On Instagram she had a follow request from a user named realMitchBennett. On Twitter, another request, this one from @realMitchBennett. She stared at her phone, wondering who would pull such a disturbing prank. Believing it to be the only way for her to find out who the hoaxer was, she accepted all the requests. When she tried to look at the profiles, there was nothing but a black screen. Further rattled by the lack of information on the social media feeds, she plugged her phone into the charger and lay back in the bed.

It was past midnight. She couldn't call Liv. There was no one she could call, no matter how badly she wanted to share the creepy events. She considered walking to the motel office to see if Iva was awake, but shut that idea down. The girl would think she was boarding an unhinged woman.

Certain she wouldn't be able to sleep with all the weirdness, she stared at the ceiling. Soon she was serenaded by an army of frogs that sounded as if they were lined up outside the bathroom window. The racket forced out all other noises and she drifted off into a dreamless sleep.

Awakened by the rush of highway traffic outside, Carly grabbed her phone from the nightstand. She'd slept through several notifications. She noticed the time. It was almost noon. The room was brightly lit, even though only a small beam of sun shone through gaps in the drawn curtain.

She checked her text messages first. There was only one from Liv.

LIV: *Bennett compound, two o'clock, DO NOT BE LATE!*

Carly groaned. Visiting her father's house was never on her list of favorite things, but she couldn't help thinking that today's visit would be worse than any in the past. She replied to her sister, assuring her that she would be there on time, and moved on to her Facebook account, where she discovered over seventy notifications. She held her breath while clicking on the heart. She didn't really use her Facebook account for much more than following old friends and hadn't posted anything herself for months. She'd also never gotten so many comments on her photos. All the comments she saw today were from the Mitch Bennett account.

Troubled by the onslaught of messages from someone claiming to be her father, she went through the motions of getting ready, all the while scrolling through the comments.

There were pictures of her with her castmates from school plays and musicals. Under each photo was a message from the supposed real Mitch Bennett, all expressing similar thoughts.

"You look so happy. I should have come to this production."

Under an image from her prom in which she wore a gown from a local thrift store, only one word from Mitch: "Stunning!"

Photo after photo, the person posing as her father interjected thoughts, mostly conveying regret, and some, pride. Carly wondered who had the time to dedicate to this project. It must have taken whomever it was hours.

As she brushed her teeth, she was getting to the last of the alerts, but was tiring of them too. She couldn't pinpoint the emotions she felt, but finally decided on anger. Anger at the person perpetrating this cruel hoax and anger at herself for wishing they could be the actual words of her father. Anger that she would let herself believe he'd ever cared enough to show up to one of her performances, to see her off on her prom date. It was too much, and she fought the urge to hurl her phone across the room.

Pushing the thoughts out of her mind, she checked her look in the mirror and grabbed her sneakers. As she tied her shoes, there was a knock on the door. Her first thought was Liv. She wouldn't put it past her sister to show up unannounced to make certain Carly didn't ditch, leaving Liv to make the trip to see her stepmother and half-siblings on her own. But when she reached the door, her hand hovered over the knob. Instead of hurling the door open or calling out to the person on the other side, she peered through the peephole. All she saw was the fish-eyed view of the worn parking lot, her car taking up most of the warped frame.

She slowly opened the door, hoping that perhaps Iva had left fresh towels. One eye peeked out the crack in the door. There was no one there. Craning her neck to get a better view of the outside, she spotted a shiny blue Mercedes parked in front of the unit a few doors down. It was backed in. *Can't imagine anyone with such a nice car would want to stay in this dive,* she thought.

She eyed the car, leaning further out of the motel room until she was almost on the walk connecting the units. She noticed the vanity plate on the Mercedes, one that was very familiar to her. It read MBS GAL; it had donned every one of Janace's Mercedes. She had a two-year rule for her cars, trading them in every other year. She always drove a Mercedes, and they always bore the plate, short for Mitch Bennett's Gal.

Just as Carly considered going back inside, Janace stepped out of the car and walked to a room a few doors down from Carly's. The room to the door opened as Janace approached. She leaned in and kissed the occupant's cheek; making an exaggerated smacking sound, kicking one of her feet back while she stood on the toe of the other foot. She held a small white paper bag, and she handed it to the man who remained outside of Carly's view.

"I won't be needing these any longer. You should probably return them to Charlene."

Although Carly hadn't got a look at the person speaking to Janace, she knew who it had to be at the mention of the name Charlene. The only Charlene she could think of was Uncle Mark's wife. The man leaned outside the room and took

Janace's wrist, pulling her in. Carly was right. It was Uncle Mark.

She quickly backed into her room and shut the door. The two didn't seem to be hiding their rendezvous any more than other people in illicit relationships did by booking a few hours at the Roadside. Uncle Mark knew Carly was staying here. Surely Janace noticed the Arizona plates on the one other car in the motel parking lot. How could they be so conspicuous? Her father's body wasn't yet cold, and Janace was at a no-tell motel with none other than Mitch's lifelong best friend. Nothing made sense.

She busied herself with checking the comments the Mitch impersonator left on her Instagram page until she heard voices outside her room. She pulled the curtain back a crack to see Janace getting into her car.

Carly would be too early if she left now, but she couldn't stand to be in the room for another minute. She made sure all the lights were on, grabbed her purse and keys and left the room, checking that the door locked behind her. Part of her wanted to run into Uncle Mark, to see how he would react coming face-to-face with her, but she fought the urge to knock on the door of the room.

She got in her car, deciding to grab some coffee before making the drive to Camelot Crossing, but as she turned the key in the ignition, she heard a click. It was the unmistakable sound of a faulty starter well. She made a few more attempts to get the car to fire up, but had no luck. As she returned to her room, she dialed her sister.

"Hey, sorry for the late notice. Car trouble. Can I bum a ride?"

———

Carly waited at the window for her sister. As soon as she saw

Liv's car pull into the parking lot, she grabbed her purse and rushed out the door.

"This works out better," Liv said before Carly shut the door.

"Good morning! Nice to see you too," Carly muttered. Liv threw the car into reverse and was turning onto the highway before Carly could buckle her seat belt. She knew it would be impossible to bring up the weird scene that played out beyond her motel room door.

"Before we enter Janace's lair, we need to go over some trigger words—"

"Trigger words?"

"Yes, trigger words." Carly saw Liv's eye roll as she pressed on. "Words you don't say around Janace to avoid some horrid political debate or off-base conspiracy rant. Trust me, this is for your own good."

"I see," Carly replied as she gazed out the window, amazed at how the landscape had changed just outside of town on Highway 51. What was once farmland now held an odd mix of car dealerships, restaurants, and medical buildings.

"Listen carefully," Liv said. "'Elections, fake news, five-G, the virus, the word 'woke.'"

Carly had to laugh at her sister as she rattled off words not to be spoken. "You've compiled quite the list."

"Don't laugh, Carly. This is important," Liv said sternly before moving on. "Let me think, um, indoctrination, the election—"

Carly lifted a finger and turned to her sister. Before she could inquire which election was off limits, Liv interrupted.

"Any election. The Supreme Court, January 6th."

Now Carly interrupted her sister. "Okay, I get it. No hot-button topics. How are the kids? Where are the kids?"

Liv turned onto Range Road and took advantage of being

away from highway traffic to take her eyes off the road for a few seconds. She looked directly at Carly and continued.

"They are fine and with a neighbor. There's one more. You absolutely cannot mention this at all under any circumstances," Liv implored.

"Hit me. Wait, let me guess."

"Carly, focus! We're almost there. Do not say anything about abortion."

"That's not one of my usual conversation starters, so I think we're safe."

As the car navigated the rolling blind hills and potholes, Carly leaned her head back and closed her eyes. While she hadn't thought about it in years, her mind traveled back to a day she knew she'd never forget.

Chapter Ten

2006

Every year before school let out for winter break, the middle school choir traveled to several elementary schools to perform their holiday concert. Carly rode the bus, laughing with her friends, swapping Santa hats and belled shoe covers as they made their way to Westwood Elementary.

The concert went well. A few snowflakes fell as the group lined up to board the bus that would take them to the next school. Carly stood at the back of the line and saw the school nurse approach her choir teacher. The two adults spoke before Mrs. Weber stood on her tiptoes and scanned the line. She made brief eye contact with Carly before pointing to the girl. The nurse made her way down the line before stopping in front of Carly.

"You Carly Bennett?" the nurse asked. "Kimmi Bennett's sister?"

"Half-sister," Carly corrected the woman.

"Half-sister will do. I'm Nurse Mann. Your sister is in my office with a nosebleed that won't stop. She's in quite a state, too. Your mother is in Tulsa and can't make it to the school for a couple of hours."

"She's not my mother."

Nurse Mann ignored this comment.

"I've cleared it with Mrs. Weber. I need you to come with me."

The line started moving, and Carly did her best to keep up.

"Well, I—" Carly stammered. "I've got to go to the concert. It's my final grade for the semester."

"I understand that, dear," Nurse Mann said, grabbing Carly's wrist and pulling her from the line. "As I said, Mrs. Weber agreed to let you stay behind to comfort your sister."

Nurse Mann didn't let go of Carly's wrist until the two had reentered the school. Carly looked back to watch the bus pull away. She still felt the need to protest the change in her schedule.

"I don't think I can help," she asserted. "We're not really close." Westwood was the school Carly attended from kindergarten through fifth grade. She was familiar with the halls and knew where the nurse's office was. Nurse Mann was new to the school.

"Nonsense," the woman retorted. "Kids are dropping left and right from this stomach bug. I can't dedicate the next couple of hours to holding her hand and trying to calm her down. Your mother—"

"Stepmother," Carly interjected. Nurse Mann ignored this response as she rushed down the hallway. A group of kids stood outside the Nurse's office, two holding trash cans. As they got near the group, Carly saw their pasty faces. *Great, guess I'm also getting the stomach flu,* she thought.

Carly stopped short of the door and Nurse Mann continued her brisk walk, stopping at the entrance to her office.

"I'll be right with you all," she said to the line of children. "I put calls in to your folks, and you'll be home in your own beds before lunch." The nurse turned back to Carly. "Ms. Bennett, please hurry."

Carly scanned the hallway, looking for someone who could help pry her away from this interruption to her day. There was no one. A kid in the line hurled into the trash can, prompting Nurse Mann to become short with Carly.

"Now, young lady!"

Carly shuffled past the sick kids and saw Kimmi behind a glass partition in the nurse's office. The child was wailing. Blood stained the front of what was once a white shirt with crisp ruffles down the front. The girl glanced up from her misery and her sobs grew louder as she spotted Carly.

"See, I told you—" Carly began.

"Nonsense! You're here now and the bus is long gone. Get in there and try to calm the poor girl down. Who's next?" the nurse called out, letting Carly know the debate was over.

"I want my mom," Kimmi groaned as Carly took a seat next to her. The girl had rolled up Kleenex wads protruding from her nostrils. Carly could see the crimson blood seeping through. *How could a nose bleed for so long?*

"Yeah, sorry, you got me," Carly said. "What's up with your nose?"

"None of your business," the girl snapped.

"Alrighty, then. Guess we'll sit here in silence. What fun! I'm missing my choir concert tour as we speak."

Kimmi did not reply. She turned away from Carly and continued to whimper. For the next hour and a half, Carly watched the school nurse dispense Band-Aids and assure parents their kid's stomach ailments would be a thing of the past in twenty-four hours. She thought Kimmi had dozed off, but the girl jumped up the second Janace entered the office.

"Mommy!" she cried, gathering up bloodied tissues.

Janace ran to Kimmi and got down on her knees, stroking the girl's face and pushing her hair back.

"My poor baby," Janace cooed. "We have no choice now, darling. We will have to make an appointment with Dr. Grant. I don't think we can avoid surgery any longer."

Kimmi let out a lengthy disapproval, dragging each word out far longer than necessary. "No, Mommy. I don't want my nose burned."

"Now, now. Dr. Grant assured us you won't feel a thing and afterwards, these nosebleeds will be a thing of the past."

It was then Janace realized the other person in the room with her daughter was Carly.

"Oh, my. What are you doing here, Carly?"

"I, um—" she began, but Nurse Mann came around the partition, sparing Carly the trouble.

"Good afternoon, Mrs. Bennett. Carly was here for the choir concert and was kind enough to sit with her sister until you could get here."

"They're half-sisters. But that was—" Janace looked up and pursed her lips. It was clear she struggled with what to say. "Kind?"

"Yes, she was a tremendous help. I'm so sorry about Kimmi's nosebleed. I've never had such trouble stopping the flow of one."

"Well, Dr. Grant wants to cauterize the blood vessels in her nostrils."

Kimmi had quieted briefly, but these words stirred her sobs.

"We've been putting off because, as you can see, she is adamant it not be done."

"Now, Kimmi, the doctor knows best," Nurse Mann said, handing the girl a sucker.

Carly realized how dry her throat was and wished she'd been offered a sucker.

"So, I guess I need to give you a ride, Carly," Janace said. "Where should I take you?"

Carly glanced at the clock that sat high on the wall. There were still two hours left in the school day. She didn't know what school the rest of the choir might be at.

"Back to the middle school, I guess."

"Well, that's quite out of our way, isn't it?"

Carly shrugged.

"We've gathered up all her belongings, coat, lunchbox, and backpack. She'll want to put that coat on. Is it still snowing?" the nurse fussed.

"Just flurries for now, but we should get a move on. I hate driving in this stuff and it's only going to get worse."

Carly followed her stepmother and half-sister out of the school. Janace had parked in the fire lane, the hazard lights of her powder blue Mercedes flashing. When they arrived at the car, Kimmi got into the front seat.

"You be careful not to get that blood on my seats now, Kimmi."

As Janace pulled the car out of the parking lot, she made eye contact with Carly in the rearview mirror.

"Do you know where I was today, Carly?"

"No, ma'am, I don't. I think the nurse said Tulsa."

"Yes, yes, I was in Tulsa and for a very important reason." Janace looked back at Carly now. "Do you know what that reason might be?"

Carly looked at the woman blankly.

"It was to stand up for the rights of the unborn!" Janace exclaimed.

Carly still had no idea what the woman was going on about.

"It is a scourge on our society, you know? One of the greatest evils on this planet. It was a wonderful protest!"

Carly had never heard protests referred to as wonderful,

but she was putting together the pieces that told her what Janace was wonderfully protesting. The woman was always an outspoken pro-lifer, something that at Carly's age she had no great interest in.

"You should be angry too, Carly," Janace continued. "Life begins at conception, and it is up to us to protect all those tiny, little souls that are ripped from their mother's bellies every single day!'

Carly looked up to see the light they approached turn yellow. She shifted in her seat, annoyed that the streetlight hadn't stayed green. All she wanted was to get out of this car.

Janace was silent as she waited for the light to turn green. She looked into her mirror and made eye contact with Carly again.

"You know, you were one of those souls that could have been lost to this world."

Carly didn't know what Janace meant, but she didn't have to wait long as the woman continued.

"Your mother wanted to abort you. Were you aware of that?"

She didn't wait for Carly to answer.

"If it weren't for your father, you wouldn't be here right now."

Janace let this news sit as Carly absorbed what she'd said. The heater was suddenly far too hot. Icy tendrils of sweat snaked down Carly's back. She was relieved to see they were turning into the middle school parking lot. Carly unbuckled her seat belt before the car came to a stop. Janace's words raged like a fire inside Carly's head. No one had ever told her that Mother had wanted to abort her, that she was unwanted. As the news settled in her heart, hot tears slid down her face. She refused to look at Janace now, not wanting the woman to see her cry.

Janace stopped the car and turned back to Carly as the girl fumbled with the lock before throwing the car door open.

"You should think about that. Maybe you'll join the fight. I mean, what kind of mother would choose to murder her baby before she'd ever cradled it in her arms?"

Carly slammed the door on Janace's words and ran to the school door, never looking back.

Chapter Eleven

2022

Liv drove slowly over the narrow bridge that crossed the pond at the entrance of Camelot Crossing. An inverted image of the budding trees shone on the water's surface. A lone egret rose weightlessly from the water and took flight, passing over the car.

The neighborhood held a mythical and wondrous quality to Carly as a child. As Liv navigated the bend dubbed "Deadman's Curve" by the residents, she wondered if what lay beyond the pass would still inspire such awe in her. She hoped she'd moved past what was likely the childhood fancy and silly allure of the rarely visited home. Her hopes were dashed as they rounded the first of the winding roads that disappeared into private drives. The neighborhood was a rarity.

Shadows danced over her face from the canopy of trees that shrouded the path. The trees were just beginning to bloom in the warmth of spring days. Pink and white buds punctuated the sea of green. By summer, the houses glimpsed between the emerging forest would be invisible from the road as the homes were tucked deep into their lots. They passed another car, and Liv raised her index finger off the steering wheel. The driver of the other car did the same, the customary passing wave of the sprawling development. Despite not spending much time in Camelot Crossing, the subtle one-finger acknowledgment was ingrained.

"You need to know that things have changed at the compound. For starters, Janace's face has had as much of a renovation as her home. The house looks different, and so does she. You can decide for yourself which new look is more repugnant."

"You know, I have some things to discuss with you, too. I didn't realize that I'd need a refresher course on how to deal with the elite."

"Carly, be serious. You should be grateful. By pointing out the potential landmines lurking beneath the facade, I am giving you a gift. Knowing how to avoid volatile subject matter, one can avoid blowing things up. Now, Rachel is pregnant again, but no one talks about it. She's been very guarded after the last pregnancy ended the way it did."

Carly nodded, hoping she'd remember all of it. Maybe she could just avoid conversations altogether.

"Of course, you know Kimmi is pregnant, too. Her pregnancy is basically the only thing she wants to talk about. Well, now that Mitch is dead, maybe she'll talk about him, too."

In the whirlwind of Liv's crash course on handling a get-together with the family, Carly had almost forgotten about the barrage of social media responses she'd received from the impostor dive-bombing her Facebook and Instagram feeds.

Liv took a break in her diatribe as they approached the private drive. Carly saw her chance and took it.

"So, have you gotten any weird friend or follow requests on your socials?"

Liv's shoulders dropped, and she looked at Carly with her lips pursed, shaking her head.

"Carls, I have a newborn and a preschooler. I don't have time to pee, much less to scroll through Instagram."

They turned onto the private lane, and the impressive Bennett compound came into view. The road ended in a roundabout. Her father's house sat in the middle of two slightly more modest, but gorgeous houses. Mitch owned four lots in this nook of Camelot Crossing, arguably the most obscure corner of the neighborhood.

Chip's house sat to the right of Mitch's, a cottage-style home made of gray stones, and punctuated by arched windows trimmed in brick. Kimmi's house was a Mediterranean Revival with creamy stucco, a terracotta tiled roof, and expansive wraparound terraces trimmed in decorative iron spindles. While all three homes were very different in design, they were surrounded by impeccable landscaping.

Liv was right about Mitch's house having changed. It was once a typical colonial home, symmetrical in every aspect aside from a windowed sunroom to one side. Originally constructed in red brick, it was now wrapped in white clapboard. The front door was punctuated by Ionic pillars. The entire facade had been remodeled to appear like a miniature version of The White House.

"Wow, you weren't kidding about the house," Carly said as the two exited the car.

"Pretty presidential, huh? Kinda creepy, in my opinion," Liv replied.

"How'd you know about the reno? I haven't been out to this house since I was in high school."

"Oh, yeah. We got invited to dinner three or four days before Christmas. There were two gifts under the tree. One for Fallon and one for Asa. It looked nothing like the picture Janace posted on Christmas Eve. That tree was so choked with gifts, it looked like it had vomited out dozens of beautifully wrapped presents. Remember, no trigger words and try not to react when you see Janace's remodeled face."

As Liv raised her hand to ring the bell, the front door opened. A crying Rachel Bennett rushed forward, almost colliding with Liv and Carly. Rachel jumped in surprise before bowing her head and pushing through the two women.

"Hey, Rachel," Liv began. "Everything okay?"

Their sister-in-law did not reply. She pushed past them and fled to her own home. Liv and Carly lost sight of her as she approached her front door.

Liv shrugged and knocked on the door left open by the fleeing pregnant woman. She stuck her head inside as she did so.

"Knock, knock, anyone home?" she called.

"Yes, in the kitchen." It was Janace's voice, falsely sweet and sticky as ever.

"Here we go. Remember what I said," Liv warned, entering the grand foyer and closing the door behind Carly.

Their footfalls echoed through the mansion as they walked through the entry hall. The wood floors gleamed in the natural light that spilled in from massive windows. The home was a jaw-dropper, like a page out of a magazine.

Janace's teacup Yorkie was the first to greet Liv and Carly. She bounded around a corner, yipping madly, baring her tiny teeth.

"Katia, quiet! We're in here, girls. Follow my voice, and my guard dog."

The kitchen was a sea of white marble. The island was a veritable smorgasbord. Along with the most gigantic charcuterie setup Carly had ever seen were bagels with a plethora of toppings, fruit baskets, bowls of salad, casseroles, and plates of cookies and cupcakes. Carly's mouth watered at the sight of the food. She'd not eaten anything since the night before.

"Hello, girls," Janace said as she poured herself a cup of coffee from a carafe on the island. "Please, please make a plate. We'll never be able to eat all this food before it spoils."

Carly grabbed a paper plate and began loading it up. Liv

went to the sunny breakfast nook just off the kitchen where Kimmi sat sobbing. A twinge of guilt clocked Carly as she stuffed a giant chocolate-covered strawberry in her mouth and heaped food onto her plate. *Guess I should've offered condolences before cramming my face full of food*, she thought.

Kimmi looked up and made eye contact with Carly. Carly gave a weak wave to her half-sister with a cheese cube in her hand. Liv was rubbing Kimmi's back and speaking softly. With a heavily loaded fruit bowl in one hand, Carly balanced a full plate on top of a coffee cup in the other and made her way to the table. Janace didn't sit down with the siblings. She busied herself picking over items spread out on the island.

"Kimmi," Janace said. "You really should eat something. You're eating for two now."

"I couldn't possibly eat, Mom. I'm far too distraught. Haven't had a bite in two days. Should help with the weigh-in at my next doctor's appointment," she finished with a faint smile.

"Appetite or no, you're going to end up in the hospital. Here, I made you a plate."

Janace crossed the room and placed it on the table in front of Kimmi. Katia shadowed the woman the entire time, settling under the chair where Janace sat. Carly got a good look at Janace's face and stomped on her own foot under the table so she wouldn't gasp. The woman's eyes stretched upwards, as if she wanted her eyebrows to meet her hairline. Her lips resembled overinflated inner tubes painted in coral lipstick. It was too much to take in at once, so she distracted herself by comparing her plate to the one given to Kimmi. While Carly's overflowed with a sampling of almost everything on the island, Kimmi's plate had three carrot sticks, some cheese slices and a banana.

"Mom, you know I can't eat bananas. My OB told me they can cause bloat." She pushed the plate away after grabbing one carrot stick.

"A doctor would deprive a pregnant woman a banana?" Liv questioned.

"Carbs, Liv. It's important for me to keep my figure, despite feeling like a whale," Kimmi snapped.

"The reason I've asked you girls over is to fill you in on the details surrounding your father's death—"

Kimmi pulled a tissue from the box sitting next to her and tossed the carrot stick back onto the plate before dabbing her eyes. Liv rubbed the woman's arm, a gesture Kimmi ignored. Janace remained composed. Aside from looking like she was in a perpetual state of shock, one would never believe she was in mourning.

"Compose yourself, dear," she issued before moving on. "As you know, the service is tomorrow. Mr. Childers would like us to all meet the following day at his office. There is a will. This meeting will likely be rescheduled, as I need some things clarified by Mr. Childers and his people."

"What things do you need clarified?" Carly asked before popping a grape in her mouth. Liv kicked her under the table.

"Nothing you should worry yourself about. I'm not trying to steal any inheritance you may have away from you."

"No, I wasn't—" Carly gave up on defending herself. She'd taken a bite out of a bagel smeared with cream cheese after asking the question.

"There are some discrepancies in the timing," Janace replied. "Obviously, I am not trying to hide anything from you. I invited you into my home, after all."

Carly vowed to herself not to say another word.

"We saw Rachel as we were coming in." Liv jumped in to change the direction of the conversation. "She seemed upset. Is she okay?"

"Oh, that girl. She's fine. Pregnancy hormones and all. She keeps herself hemmed into her house. It's like pulling teeth to get her to join us and when she does, she inevitably gets upset about something and shuts down."

"Well, she has to feel guilty. Daddy died on her watch. Some nurse's aide she is," Kimmi said.

"Now, Kimmi. Your father's death wasn't any fault of hers. The man had been sick for days. Couldn't even get out of bed. Stubbornness killed Mitch Bennett, along with his refusal to see a doctor. Lord knows I tried to take him to the hospital. The man wouldn't budge. If anything, it'd be my fault. I shouldn't have left him in that state, but I really couldn't miss a pro-life rally that I myself organized. That just wouldn't look right."

Liv saw the look on Carly's face at the mention of the anti-abortion rally and scrunched her lips, raising her eyebrows and bugging her eyes, a look telling her to keep quiet.

"Maybe if I'd known how bad he was, I could have gotten through to him," Kimmi said before breaking down in sobs.

"Kimmi Jacobs, stop that talk. No one was getting through to your father, no one." Janace pressed her palms into the table, closed her eyes and took a deep breath. The silence made Carly want to crawl under her chair.

"Momma, look at the time," Kimmi said.

"Oh goodness, you're right." Janace glanced at her watch. "Sorry to chase you girls off, but we have a meeting at the funeral home in fifteen minutes. We'll never make it on time."

"I've got the afternoon free," Liv said. "Should we join you?"

"That won't be necessary. We're just going over a few of the arrangements with the director. Now that the ashes are ready, we need to pick out—" Janace stopped herself short.

"Pick out what?" Carly questioned.

"If you must know, we need to select an urn. Uncle Mark graciously volunteered to witness the cremation. It was truly a godsend. He spared us that arduous task. Now that it is done, we want to pick out an urn Mitch would be happy with. We're running very short on time, given that the service is tomorrow." Janace rose from the table and pushed her chair in.

"Forgive me for asking," Carly said, rising from her chair, breaking the promise she'd made to herself only moments earlier. "But I thought Father was against cremation."

"At one time he was. People change, Carly. It's been some time since you've seen your father. These were his wishes and I refuse to go against them." Janace turned her back on Carly and said, "Kimmi, text Rachel and ask her to come put this food away while we're gone. We simply don't have the time to clean up right now."

"Carly and I can take care of it," Liv offered.

"That won't be necessary. Rachel has a key and knows the security code. If you girls will just see yourselves out, we'll go through the garage and lock the doors remotely."

Carly took her plate to the trash can and reluctantly dumped half of the food into the bin. Liv approached and handed Carly her purse.

"I need to make a quick stop in the restroom, and then we'll be on our way," Liv said. "So much for reminiscing. What'd she give us, ten minutes?"

"I could sum up my Mitch memories in half that time," Carly replied.

The two made their way toward the front door. Just beyond the entry was a powder room.

"I'll be quick," Liv promised. Carly waited outside the small study near the home's entrance, but was drawn in by the room's contents. The walls were adorned with countless family photos. Mitch, his wife and two youngest kids with Mickey Mouse, in the sea surrounded by dolphins, on skis atop a snowy mountain. The four beaming in every shot. There were also school photos. Janace clustered each child's school pictures together, preschool through graduation. One wall held more formal family photos. The foursome in matching outfits at Theta Pond, and wearing all orange at Pickens Stadium.

There were candid shots as well of the kids in the swimming pool, riding horses, and of course many of Chip in football uniforms and Kimmi in her cheerleading skirts. Pictures of Kimmi's kids, Nora and Cole, spanning from their newborn photos to more recent ones, sat on the bookcases. In another, Mitch, Janace, their two kids, the spouses and grandchildren in complementary shades of blue, all smiled from the white sands of a Florida beach. The photographic history was dizzying, and neither she nor Liv appeared in any of them.

She moved slowly, taking in every photo displayed. The temperature in the small room plummeted. Carly rubbed her arms as goosebumps popped up and an icy chill skittered down her spine. She looked up to see if she had stepped under an air-conditioning vent when she heard a voice coming from behind her. She spun, already embarrassed to be caught in the room she had no right to be in. There was no one there, but she glimpsed the shadow of a person beyond the threshold of the room. She'd turned to follow the person when a crash followed by the tinkling of glass broke the silence, causing her to jump. A photo had fallen off the wall near the doorway to the study. Carly searched her surroundings again.

How would she explain this? Should she just bail and hope no one was ever the wiser? This option evaporated from her mind when she saw the photo that had fallen. It was the Bennett family in matching Christmas pajamas. The holiday PJ image wasn't what caught her attention though. The Christmas picture had been placed over another image; one of Carly, Liv and Father. She slid the picture out of the shattered frame, being careful not to cut herself on the shards of glass. She was certain she'd never seen this photo before, but judging by her age, she believed it had to be before Mitch married Janace.

Footfalls approached in the hall. Without thinking, she carefully tucked the photo into her purse.

"Carly, what are you doing in here?" Liv hissed. "Oh my God, did you knock that frame off the wall?"

"No, it um, fell. I was just looking," Carly replied. "Let's get out of here." She couldn't tell Liv that someone might have seen her in the room, remembering the shadow that slipped by. Maybe it was a housekeeper or something.

"Why is it so cold in here? Should we clean this mess up?" Liv asked. "No, on second thought, let's leave it. Maybe they won't think it was us. Come on, let's go."

The two women rushed out of the house and hurried to the car. As they pulled away, one of the four garage doors on the side of the house opened. The same Mercedes Carly saw in the Roadside parking lot emerged. At the same time, Carly saw Rachel exit her house and make her way to Janace's. The woman was so small, one wouldn't know she was pregnant by looking at her.

"Hey, did you get a package of photos a couple of years ago from Janace?" Carly asked as a memory crept to the front of her mind.

"Oh, yeah, I did. It was odd, right? Who returns pictures of their kids to their kids? Like Mitch could forget his two oldest daughters existed just because he got rid of a box of photos?"

Chapter Twelve

2020

Carly flipped through her mail, quite a large stack since she hadn't checked the locked box at the complex entry for some time. The advertising agency she worked for had shifted to remote work at the beginning of the pandemic. There was no word on when they would be back to normal. In the absence of the work-home-work routine, she often forgot she had a mailbox.

She shuffled through the junk mail disinterestedly until one envelope grabbed her attention. She took the stairs two at a time and fumbled clumsily with her keys to unlock the front door. When she entered the apartment, she let the fliers and bills fall to the floor, leaving a sprawl of paper she stepped on as she hurried to her desk to get her letter opener. There was no mistaking who the package was from. Her stepmother had impeccable penmanship, bubbly letters all reaching exact levels of height and depth, each cursive word easy to read. Carly only received mail from her stepmother twice a year: a generic birthday card with a twenty-dollar bill and an equally generic Christmas greeting that held a fifty-dollar bill. Each piece of currency was always fresh, crisp, and creaseless, and her father's name was always signed in the same flowery penmanship of his wife.

This letter was different, not only due to the timing, far too early for her October birthday, too late for Christmas. She was certain she'd never received an eight-and-a-half by eleven-inch manila envelope from Janace; this package had some weight to it as well. It was adorned with an abundance of American flags, from the three stamps in one corner to Janace's patriotic, personalized mailing label on the other. A sense of dread washed over her as the razor-sharp opener made a hissing sound, slicing the package open in a neat line. She wasn't sure why she felt uneasy; she just did. It was the same type of alarm she might feel if she were to get a call in the wee hours of the morning before the sun came up. This could not be good news.

She closed her eyes and reached blindly into the envelope, her fingers first falling on a thick, slippery piece of paper. With trembling hands, she withdrew the note— Janace's personal stationery, which matched her mailing label. On it were two sentences in the woman's unmistakable, elegant script.

Hi Carly -

Your Dad and I are going through old pictures and thought you might want these. They're really old!

Sincerely, Janace Bennett

Carly felt the tension leaving her body; at least it wasn't bad news. She let the festive letterhead drift to the floor. Inside she found several photos, and Janace was correct; they were old. Carly recognized them as the same photos that hung on the walls of her childhood home. These photos, however, held their original vibrant color and glossy sheen. They had obviously been stowed away in a box, not hung on a wall to be weathered by time and the sun. One was still encased in a paper frame made to look like woodgrain. Two were obviously school pictures, the stock mottled-gray backdrop a dead give-away. The other evidence was her look. In one, a cowlick protruded from a plastic hair clip, and in the other she could tell her bangs were freshly cut by the unsteady hand of her mother. Her thick, shiny brown hair framed her face unevenly; her smile was distant. She was the spitting image of her father.

The third photo was more unique. Looking at the picture of her younger sister and herself, she was cast back to the day the photo was taken. She and Liv wore matching green velvet vests with frilly white shirts. The shirts had puff sleeves cinched in lace at the wrists and tiny bows at the neck. She remembered Liv's tights pooled in wrinkled puddles at her ankles, and she helped her little sister pull them up when they arrived at the Sears Appliance Center on Main Street. A few times a year, the washer-dryer sets and deep freezers were pushed back to make way for a photography station. The people from Olan Mills worked day and night snapping baby's first photos and family portraits while anxious moms hoped everyone smiled and no one's eyes were closed.

She and Liv waited patiently in line while their mother stepped into the cold air and watched them from outside the storefront window while she smoked. Cheery Christmas tunes jangled from overhead speakers. Carly and Liv spun on one foot in dizzying circles to see whose skirt could billow up the biggest, and which twisted more grandly around their bodies when they came to a sudden stop. They held each other and leaned on a row of dishwashers to keep from toppling over or bumping into others waiting in line, both giggling madly as the room stopped spinning and blurry double vision became focused. Carly had looked up to find her mother staring at them through the plate glass, fogging the window some, but not enough for Carly to mistake her mother's gesturing wordlessly to stop by running her finger across her neck.

The two giddy girls entertained themselves next by tap-dancing in their shoes, shiny black faux-patent Mary Janes. When they were next in line, they checked each other's matching hairdos for fly-aways and errant strands. The two were reverse negatives of each other, Carly with her tan complexion, brown locks and green eyes, and Liv with her fair skin, blond hair, and blue orbs. Their mother rushed in just in time for the haggard photographer to call out the name Bennett in a dispirited tone. This was before their mother gave up, before her addictions became the most important thing in her world. It was the last time Carly and Liv had a professional photo taken together, a photo their father never bothered to hang on his walls. She figured Liv had the sun-faded duplicate carefully stored in its plastic wood-look frame with gold gilding tucked away in a closet. Now Carly had the other copy, her father apparently done with it.

Chapter Thirteen

2022

Liv dropped Carly back at the Roadside, and Carly immediately set about finding a tow service. She'd have the car towed to her father's repair shop, mostly because it was the only one she knew that was still in business. While waiting for the tow truck, she got a text notification.

FATHER: *You're right about the starter. Have the radio and window looked at too.*

She dropped her phone as if it'd burned her hands. She'd told no one about her suspicions that the car's starter was blown; at least she didn't remember mentioning it to Liv. But she was certain she hadn't spoken of the issues with the radio or the window. Who could've known these things?

The walls of the tiny motel room pushed in on her as her mind grappled with the implications of the latest text message. She couldn't think of anyone who held such a grudge against her that they'd devote so much time to creating social media accounts, comment on all of her photos, and torment her with beguiling text messages. Maybe Chip; but he had a job and a pregnant wife. It didn't seem likely he'd waste the time. Plus, she didn't believe him to be tech-savvy enough to pull a stunt like this off. His limited posts and social media interactions were clumsy and weird. Kimmi would never dedicate enough to time to someone other than herself to torment her half-sister. And Janace… The woman's social media feeds were a bizarre collection of prayer requests, political conspiracies, racially derogatory memes, calls to build a wall and ban books, and of course, pro-life rants. The type of stuff most people roll their eyes at and scroll on past. She only used Facebook and viewed the forum as a way to let the world know that, in her opinion, she was most definitely on the right side of every cause.

Feeling the need for fresh air, Carly decided she would move outside to wait on the tow truck. A cold snap had settled over Oklahoma that evening. She grabbed her hoodie and phone and sat on the curb outside the room. The same car that was in the lot when she first arrived was parked by the office. A light shone in the lobby window, and she considered waiting with Iva, mostly so she wasn't alone. That idea was tossed aside as she dwelled on the strange happenings.

She went to her Facebook page and scrolled through the dozens of comments made by the Mitch Bennett impostor, hoping she might find a clue in the messages. If there were any hints to the poster's identity, she couldn't decipher them. The words were all things her father might have commented had he taken the time to look at her profile.

As the sun dipped below the horizon, the tow truck pulled into the parking lot. The driver made quick work of loading her car onto his truck, and within minutes, the task was complete. She kicked herself for not having Liv take her to get some dinner or snacks. The food she ate at Janace's house wasn't enough to stave off hunger for the rest of the night. *Guess I'll be eating from the vending machines tonight,* she thought as she turned the key in the door.

Before she swung the door open, the television came to life

inside the room. This time what appeared on the screen wasn't an old movie; it was an advertisement. While people in complementary shades of teal danced about, an announcer screamed over the music.

"Keppera is used to treat epileptic seizures. Side effects may cause—"

Carly grabbed the comforter while the announcer rattled off a vast list of side effects.

"... aggression, abnormal behavior, mistrust, rapidly changing moods..."

She was about to drown the noise with the comforter when the commercial ended and the television snapped off.

"That's it," she said to the empty room. "I'm outta here."

She went about packing up her belongings, peeking under the bed and checking the drawers, knowing there was nothing there but looking just in case. She set her bags by the door of the room and adjusted the thermostat off of frigid, then turned all the lights off for the first time since she'd turned them on. She felt bad about leaving a mess and extra laundry for Iva, but she couldn't stay in the room another second.

She closed the door behind her and walked to the office. Iva was engrossed in something on the computer screen when Carly entered.

"Hey, Carly, how's it going?" Iva's cheeks flushed and she turned the monitor to the wall. "Please don't tell Mr. Watts, I was just playing solitaire. I need something to keep me awake."

"Your secret is safe with me," Carly replied with a wink.

"Did you need something? Oh, are you checking out already?" the girl said as she noticed Carly set her bags down.

"No, not checking out, but I would like to switch rooms. I'm really sorry, but I think there's something wrong with the television in my room."

"Oh?"

"Yeah, it keeps powering on at random, and the remote control also has a mind of its own."

"Hmmm, weird."

"Yeah, I thought I could live with it, but it's getting too annoying," Carly said with a nervous laugh.

"Sure, I get it. Well, all the other rooms are still available, so take your pick."

"I think I'll take the one next door. I feel kind of like I'm in no-man's-land down there on the end."

"Sure thing." Iva turned to the computer and began typing. "Let me just change some things here in the system—"

"I'm really sorry to generate laundry for you and that the room will have to be cleaned. I promise I'm not usually—"

"No worries," Iva laughed. "My brother comes in to do the cleaning and upkeep. He'll be happy to have something to do. Okay, you're all set. Here's your new room key. Let me know if you need anything else."

"Great, thanks so much," Carly replied, trading keys with the girl.

"Hope this room treats you better!"

"Me too!" Carly said as she left the office.

It was full dark now, and Carly was getting hungry. She entered the room, set her things down, and pulled her wallet from her purse. Next, she went to the vending machines and bought a bag of pretzels and a granola bar, along with a soda and a bottle of water.

Back in the new but nearly identical room, she tried leaving the television on so it wouldn't startle her should it behave as the last one did. She kicked her shoes off and did a belly flop on the bed, her snacks and soda in arm's reach, and channel surfed. She was relieved that the remote worked, but soon noticed something odd. Each time she landed on a different station, the same commercial she'd just seen in the old room came on. *Seems like excessive traffic for one ad,* she thought. Having worked in advertising for several years, she wondered how much the drugmaker was paying for such heavy rotation.

Before long, her eyes grew heavy, and she got ready for bed. She left the television on as she slept. The jingle from the Keppera ad had become an irritating ear worm.

Her sleep was interrupted by her phone moments after she'd pushed the song out of her head and was nodding off. With bleary eyes, she opened her text messages, certain it would be from Liv. Instead, she saw it was from her father's impersonator.

FATHER: *Don't ignore the clues. They will lead you to the truth. Sweet dreams.*

She pushed the phone back to the nightstand, the words in the message swimming madly in her mind as she stared at the popcorn ceiling. Clues? The truth? The truth about what?

Sleep was elusive. She pulled the remote from its Velcro nest and channel surfed again in an effort to quiet her thoughts and questions. Station after station broadcast only one thing, the unnerving advertisement for a drug that before today, she'd never heard of.

In frustration, she groaned and snapped the television off, tossing the remote aside. She grabbed the pillow next to her and covered her ears with it.

Chapter Fourteen

2022

Faint light peeked through the gaps around the heavy curtains as Carly woke. She jumped out of bed and opened the curtains. She hoped light might cast out the shadows she felt swirling around her. Throughout the night disturbing dreams fought with her sleep, and she felt anything but rested. Thick clouds shrouded the sun, so she resorted to turning on every light in the room.

In the bathroom mirror, the results of a sleepless night were written on her face, her eyes heavy with dark circles, her skin lifeless and dull.

"This is going to take some work," she said to the empty bathroom. "Today's the big day. The day we say goodbye to Mitch Bennett."

She spit toothpaste into the sink and heard her phone ringing. Sprinting back into the main room, she caught the caller just before it pushed to voice mail. She didn't recognize the number and for a fleeting moment she regretted answering the phone. What if the person sending her texts were reaching out? She didn't have time to process the thoughts.

"Hello, this is Carly."

"Ms. Bennett?" the caller asked.

"Yes."

"Trevor Anderson from Bennett Automotive."

Carly's entire body relaxed, and a knot of nervous energy escaped her lips in a long sigh.

"Yes, hi, Trevor. I hope you have good news."

"Well, ma'am, in my line of work, I'm rarely the bearer of good news, but in your case, the news could be much worse," he said with a chuckle.

"Great, how bad is it?" she asked, holding her breath.

"Well, it is the starter. Shouldn't cost too much. Your dad has you on the list of people who are only charged cost. Sorry for your loss. Mitch was a great boss. He's gonna be missed."

Carly paced the room and stared out the window as Trevor spoke. She wished he'd just get to the meat of the findings. She wasn't interested in condolences.

"Thank you, Trevor. So, how bad is the damage, and when can I get my car back? I need to head back to Phoenix the day after tomorrow."

"Think you'll have to push your trip out a little. We don't carry the parts for the repair. Need your okay to order them."

"Yes, please do. How long will it take?" she said, wrapping the curtain string around her finger.

"It'll take at least three or four days. Hate to say it, but the supply chain issues are still very real. I'll do my best to shop around and see if I can get them here any faster."

She fell to the bed and disappointment pushed against her. Her desire to leave town as soon as the will was read bordered on desperation. Maybe all the weirdness that she'd experienced since starting the journey home would disappear once she was hundreds of miles away.

"Ma'am, you there still? Sorry to—"

"No, I mean, yes. I'm still here and, of course, I understand it isn't your fault. I'd just hoped to leave as soon as I could. Well, please go ahead and do the work. Can't leave town without it. Oh, and while you're at it, can you take a look at the stereo? I think there's a bad fuse or something. And the driver's side window. I can't roll it down. Keep me posted, and thank you."

"You bet. Have a nice day ... well, nice day, considering."

She ended the call and noted the time. Liv would be hounding her soon. She'd need a ride to the service and didn't want to hold her sister up. She sent a quick text to Liv before taking a shower.

———

The crowd of people attending Mitch Bennett's funeral was staggering. Carly wondered if her father had actually touched all of their lives, or if many of the gathered mourners were here because he had almost been small-town royalty.

Derek dropped Liv and Carly off at the church entrance, the same place where Mitch and Janace tied the knot so many years ago.

"I hope he can find a parking spot. The service is going to start soon," Liv fretted.

"Yeah, we should go find seats. Looks like it's going to be standing room only in there."

Liv took Carly's hand and led her through the crowd.

"We don't have to worry about finding seats. We're going to sit with the family. They'll be through here," she said, leading Carly down an empty corridor just off the grand entrance of the church.

Liv knocked gently on the family room door as Carly protested.

"Liv," she whispered. "I don't think they are going to want us in there."

"Why not? We're family. We knew him long before anyone else in there did," Liv replied. Tears welled in her eyes, and her voice cracked. Carly felt horrible for upsetting her.

The door opened and Chip poked his head out.

"Just let us know when it's time for us to take—" Chip started before stopping himself. It was obvious he expected someone other than his two half-sisters to be on the other side of the door.

"Hey, Chip," Liv started. "Sorry we are a few minutes late. There's quite the turnout."

"Yeah, right," Chip replied. "I thought you were Pastor Allen. Wait here. Let me get my mom."

He shut the door, leaving Liv and Carly in the hallway.

"What was that?" Liv asked, clearly stumped by her half-sibling's reaction.

"I told you. They don't want us to sit with them, Liv. Let's just go find seats. We can save one for Derek." Carly tugged at her sister's arm. Liv wouldn't budge.

"Did he just?" Liv started, tears spilling down her face. "How dare he?"

Carly watched her sister and identified every emotion register on her face as they transitioned from sadness to shock to anger. Voices rose beyond the door and Liv turned from Carly, fire in her eyes. She was ready to put Chip in his place, or probably at least believed she could. Carly knew this wasn't going to end well.

The sisters heard conspiratorial whispers on the other side of the door.

"We're going in there now," Liv hissed, turning the doorknob.

The door opened, dragging Liv's hand with it.

"Oh, girls," Janace said. "I wasn't expecting you."

"Why not?" Liv said, her words expelled with angry breath. "We're his daughters, Janace. Did you think we wouldn't attend our father's funeral?"

Carly squeezed Liv's hand, and her sister pulled away.

"Of course," Janace replied, opening the door wider. "Come inside. It's almost time to take our seats."

Liv straightened her back, swiped tears from her face and entered the room with a stride that oozed confidence. Carly walked behind her, wishing she could just go find a pew in the back and ride out this nightmare there. She spotted Uncle Mark nervously shifting his hat from hand to hand across the room. Liv went directly to Kimmi while Carly made a beeline for Uncle Mark. Before she uttered a word to him, Pastor Allen entered the room.

"My dear Bennett family. I'm sorry for your loss," he said, making his way to Janace. "Mitch was so loved. There are so many here to say their goodbyes." He took Janace's hand.

"Thank you, Pastor Allen," she said before pulling a tissue from her jacket pocket and dabbing an invisible tear.

"Shall we get started?" he asked.

As if by some magical cue, the organ in the chapel began. The low murmur of the crowd beyond the door faded. Pastor Allen led Janace out. Kimmi, Chip, and their spouses fell in behind. Uncle Mark looped arms with Carly and Liv as the three took up the rear of the procession.

Carly did her best to keep her head down and not make eye contact with anyone in the pews. Uncle Mark led them to a row directly behind Janace and her children. Derek spotted Liv and met her on the far side of the pews, taking a seat next to her. Giant bouquets and sprays filled the pulpit. Sitting amid the sea of flowers was an easel holding up a large image of Mitch Bennett. The photo didn't look very recent. Next to his image sat an ornate urn holding what remained of the larger-than-life man.

Following the services, Liv insisted Carly stand with her and Derek in the family line. Minutes felt like hours as they shook hands with many of the people who came to see the great Mitch Bennett off. Carly shifted her weight as her heels grew tighter each minute. When the crowd thinned, Janace directed her brood to a limousine waiting outside. Liv stepped up to get in the car as well, but the driver closed the door before she could. She stood on the curb, mouth agape. Derek took her hand, and the three walked to his car. The limo departed before Derek could catch up to it, so he slid his vehicle into the procession as soon as he saw an opening. The three sat in silence as they drove to the cemetery.

Derek parked in the snaking line of cars and got out to open Liv's door. He took her arm and guided her toward the waiting mourners. Carly walked behind them at her own pace. She watched Liv push through the crowd and take a seat in the front, next to Rachel and Kimmi. Carly had no desire to sit next to the women, so she slowed her pace even more. As she walked through the cemetery, toward the huddled crowd, she glanced down a row of graying headstones and her eyes fell upon a familiar marker. The sense of spotting a familiar face unexpectedly in a crowd struck her. It wasn't a face, however, but her mother's resting place. The simple etched stone was more recognizable to her now than her mother's face would be. She paused for a minute in front of the stone before making her way to the Bennett mausoleum. The sun was just beginning its descent, and Carly couldn't help but notice that the grand resting place where the Bennetts would be interred created a heavy shadow that engulfed her mother's tomb.

Chapter Fifteen

2022

As Derek drove through the winding streets of Camelot Crossing, he stopped the car to allow a group of deer to cross the road. A mother deer nudged her young fawn along on its wobbly legs.

The entire Bennett cul-de-sac was packed with cars.

"This day is never going to end," Carly lamented from the backseat.

Liv ignored her and pointed out a parking space near the house. The three made their way up the expansive front walk. Every light inside and out was aglow. Despite the illumination, the dark forest edged out the ambiance beyond the large home.

They approached the front door. Murmurs and laughter of a large party spilled out. Carly wished badly that the car repairs were complete. She wasn't up to another few hours of mingling and listening to stories about her father.

Liv opened the door, and they shuffled into the full house. More floral arrangements filled the entry hall and formal living room. Servers dressed in white shirts, bow ties and vests balanced silver trays loaded with wine glasses and hors d'oeuvres as they wound their way through the throngs of people. Soft, classical music whispered from the surround sound.

"This looks more like a gala than a funeral reception," Derek whispered under his breath.

"I agree," Carly replied. "Seems a tad gauche to me."

"You two behave!" Liv hissed. Her soft melancholy smile never left her face. "To think I almost brought a casserole," Liv said, her smile widening for a flash. "Talk about gauche."

A server approached the group with wine and they declined, each of them having a reason not to imbibe: Derek being their driver, Liv being a nursing mom, and Carly fearing she'd overdo it, loosening her tongue.

As Carly took in the scene, she looked for familiar faces. Derek was quicker than she was.

"Not sure why I feel the need to schmooze with mourners, but that guy there," Derek said, pointing out a man who grabbed a wineglass from a passing server. "He's the new hospital director. I should go introduce myself."

Liv was the next to spot persons of interest.

"Look at those two," she said, tilting her head slightly to her right. "They're always thick as thieves. It's weird."

"Who? Rachel and Lance?" Carly asked.

"Yes, she hardly speaks to anyone, but put her in a room with Kimmi's husband and she's glued to him."

"I'm sure being a Bennett in-law is no walk in the park. Janace is always willing to remind people of their station. You know she doesn't think either of them is good enough for her precious children."

"Good point, but I still find their bond more than a bit sus."

"Weren't you the one who just reminded me to behave? Looks like he's upset her," Carly said.

Rachel pulled her arm away from Lance's grasp. For a minute, Carly was certain her sister-in-law was going to slap her brother-in-law. Liv grabbed Carly's hand. Her jaw dropped. Instead of slapping the man, Rachel turned and walked away, disappearing down one of the hallways that jutted off the formal space. Lance glanced around nervously. It was apparent he was looking to see if anyone noticed the discord between the two.

"Look away, look away," Liv uttered under her breath. She turned her head but side-eyed Lance.

A server approached the man, and he turned them away by shaking his head.

"That was weird," Carly said, losing Lance to a crowd of people who passed by, blotting out her view. "You better go rescue your husband. It looks like Mrs. Myers is trying to show him a something on her neck. I need to make a pit stop."

"Oh, no! The poor man is always on call, even when he's not. It's the worst of both worlds," Liv quipped as she left her sister's side and rushed to rescue her husband.

A long line formed outside the downstairs powder room. Carly didn't intend to wait, especially when it meant she'd have to explain who she was and why she was there. Instead, she ducked down a side hallway in search of another restroom. Nothing looked familiar to her. It was obvious the original house had been gutted and changed. But she continued down the hall until something caught her eye. A man opened a door at the end of the hallway. He turned to Carly, and she froze. The person was Mitch Bennett. He turned away from Carly and beckoned her to follow with the wave of his arm.

She didn't want to pursue him. All she wanted to do was run. He turned a corner, and she was powerless to ignore him. Picking up her pace, the noise of the party died in her ears. There was only her and her father. *How can this be?* she thought. Her mind struggled to make sense of what she was seeing.

She rounded the corner to see him disappear through another door. She rushed after him and found herself in the main suite of the house. Her father was gone. She searched the shadows, needing to find him. As she came around the bed, a trash can tipped over, its contents spilling onto her feet. A small scream escaped her lips, and she jumped back. She was certain she'd not knocked the wastebasket over. The bin was at the head of the bed, while she stood at the foot.

She riffled through the remnants of the bin with her foot. There were countless discarded tissues, dozens of empty blister packs from cold medicine, some bottles of eye drops and nose spray, and a lone prescription bottle. While reluctant to dig through garbage, especially the waste from a man who was reported to have died of the virus, she felt compelled to nab the transparent orange bottle. She bent to retrieve it and noticed the contents of the trash can that hadn't spilled out— more nose sprays, balled up tissue, and some empty Gatorade bottles, but no more prescription containers.

She brought the bottle to her eyes, squinting to make out the words in the dim light. She'd forgotten about her father for a moment, and nearly dropped it when she read the word out loud. "Keperra," she gasped. Instinctively, she tucked the bottle into her jacket pocket when the lights came up, casting out the darkness.

"What are you doing in here?" came a voice from behind her.

Carly's awareness was too muddled to identify who spoke. She turned to find Janace. The woman's face was red, her eyes afire.

"Carly, answer me! I thought I was more than generous to let you and your sister breach the family room and sit with us today, but this is too much!"

"I'm sorry," Carly stammered.

Janace moved toward Carly.

"Did you make this mess?" she said, eyeing the spilled bin and its contents scattered about the floor. "This is my room, and you are not welcome! Get out!"

Carly stumbled past the woman, unable to speak. Her mind screamed at her to apologize again, but her lips couldn't form the words. She fled down the hall, past the bathroom she now forgot she needed to use. In the living room, she pushed through a group of people conversing by a set of French doors that opened into the backyard. She fled, and once outside, leaned against the wall and tried to catch her breath. She peered back into the window to see if Janace had followed her, but couldn't spot the woman.

She berated herself for her actions. So childish. How would she ever explain what happened to Janace? She should have told her stepmother that she'd gotten lost. Perhaps had seen a guest go into the room and heroically gave chase to thwart a robbery. She could have said she was curious about the thread count of father's sheets. Anything besides running like a thief herself. She knew she had to do something and do it quick. Otherwise, she'd be too humiliated to look Janace in the face again. A brief text to apologize and explain might do the trick. She took out her phone.

CARLY: *Hey Janace, sorry about the run-in in your room. I got lost trying to find another restroom and wound up where I shouldn't have been. Then you scared me and, well, fight or flight...*

She reread the text five times, deciding it was the best she could come up with. Closing her eyes and holding her breath, she hit send. While she waited for a reply from her stepmother, she took in her surroundings. It had been so long since she'd been in the backyard at her father's house. It was a sprawling wonderland with a pool, a putting green, a playground, and tennis court.

The temperature had plummeted with the setting sun, the air dense with chilly moisture. A cloud of fog floated just above the pool and fell on her body with a weight that left her shivering. Clouds drifted and swirled around the full moon, painting murals on the night sky. A daddy longlegs crossed her path. She watched in awe of the impossible physics of the bulbous-bodied arachnid holding itself up on spindly legs as it moved across the patio.

From the edge of the forest, a figure emerged. The air on the veranda got colder. She wrapped her arms around herself. In the distance, she could hear a pack of coyote howling in harmony. She leaned forward, squinting her eyes, but couldn't make out who the approaching person might be, certain it was a man. As he moved across the expansive backyard, she recognized the gait. It was her father. Her heart pounded loudly as a chill ran through her. She wanted to yell at him to leave her alone and flee back into the house, but she was powerless to do so, too mesmerized by what she saw.

Her father stepped out of the shadows and beckoned for her again with the wave of his hand. She wasn't sure what was happening, but she knew there was no way she would be following her dead father into the forest. As she watched, his figure diminished. He didn't back away, or turn to leave, but faded from her sight. At that moment, she felt a hand on her shoulder and nearly jumped out of her skin, gasping, fearful of turning around. A small whimper escaped her.

"Hey, young lady, what are doing out here alone? It's pretty chilly tonight."

She closed her eyes and took a deep breath before turning toward the voice. It was Uncle Mark, and she'd never been so relieved to see the man.

"Uncle Mark!" She turned and hugged him.

"Well, now, that's what I call a welcome. Ease up, Carls, you're going to crush me," he joked.

"Sorry," Carly said, releasing him from her embrace. "I just, well—" She was bordering on tears, the first she'd cried since learning of her father's death.

"What do you say we get out of here? I've heard the same ol' Mitch Bennett stories about a hundred times today."

"You have no idea how badly I want to leave. Let me go tell Liv I've got a ride."

"I'll meet you out front," he replied.

Chapter Sixteen

2022

Carly stepped out the front door and spotted Uncle Mark. She opened the back door of his car but then saw no one sat in the front passenger seat.

"No Aunt Charlene?" Carly asked.

"No, she doesn't get out much these days. Ever since the stroke, she's been having seizures. Doctors have tried every medication under the sun to get them controlled. She hated to miss your dad's service, but a crowd that size is too overwhelming for her."

Carly shut the back door and moved to the front.

"Oh, that's right. Liv told me she had a stroke. I'm so sorry. Please give her my best," she said while buckling her seat belt.

"Will do."

The two made small talk on the short drive to the Roadside. They arrived to a parking lot with a lone car and a twitching *Vacancy* sign. Warm light shone through the window of the office.

"What say we go inside for a nightcap? I've been using the

upstairs office as my headquarters since all that social distancing nonsense hit. Don't mind saving on the rent for an office space downtown though. I'll let you in on a little secret … I keep a well-stocked liquor cabinet up there."

"Sounds like appropriate workplace conditions," she jabbed.

Inside the lobby, Iva sat, deeply engrossed in something on her phone. She glanced up with a smile that vanished when she saw her boss walk in.

"Caught ya!" Mark said.

Concern flashed in Iva's eyes. Carly felt bad for her and hoped he would let the poor girl off the hook quickly.

"Oh, sorry, Mr. Watts, I—"

"Just joshing! Gotta do something to keep from falling asleep on nights like these. I'm sure you don't believe me, but as soon as football season rolls around, you'll find yourself with your hands full, even late into the night. This place stays afloat on a few unsavory practices, but come fall, it'll be packed," he said with a wink.

Iva gave a halfhearted chuckle.

"Iva has been taking great care of this dump and me," Carly chimed in.

"Yeah, found a good one in this kid. Her brother's a keeper too. We'll be up in my office if you need anything, Iva."

Iva nodded, and the two made their way up a narrow flight of creaky stairs. This was the only upper level in the hotel and Carly didn't think she'd ever been up there. When they reached the top of the stairs, he pulled a key ring from his pocket, quickly found the one he was looking for, and unlocked the door.

"Iva and her brother have been through the wringer over the past few years. Glad to hear she's doing well. Char and I really wanted to give her a leg up. She and her brother are trying to get a place of their own to get themselves out from under a rather overbearing guardian. I'm letting them live in the apartment down there off the lobby. Wish I could do more. The whole family is in shambles. You probably heard about a few bodies found out there in Camelot Crossing?"

"I have heard a few unsavory bits. A child found buried beneath a pool and woman's remains found in the woods. Pretty creepy!" Carly replied with a shiver. "Not the kind of stuff that increases your property value."

"Definitely not. There are still questions about all of it, but one of the bodies found out in Mitch's neighborhood was Iva and Marlow's mother. What a mess. Story for another day."

He pushed the door open, and Carly was surprised to see that Uncle Mark's office was decorated much more than she'd expected. It looked more like a lodge than an office in a shady no-tell motel. The walls were covered in his "kill." The glassy eyes of mounted deer heads, turkey, and fish stared down from their plaques. The flashing *Vacancy* sign gave life to the gaze of a large wild boar's head, making the animal look more menacing than it likely had in life. Carly found them disturbing and wondered how anyone could work with so many things watching through dead eyes.

"Make yourself at home," he said as he hung his cowboy hat on a hook and made his way to the bar cart. "What's your poison?"

Carly sat on a tufted leather couch and immediately took her heels off. She rubbed her aching toes, grateful to have shed at least one of the uncomfortable items she'd been wearing all day. "I'll have what you're having."

A rush of panic washed over her as she thought back to what she saw between him and Janace the day before. She'd been thrown off-kilter, trying to wrap her mind around what their relationship might have been. He had always been a source of comfort and security. Now she'd let her guard down. His warmth could be hiding something despicable. Her eyes darted around the room as she looked for anything that might, well, she wasn't sure, prove or disprove the trusted man wasn't all she believed him to be. She reached in her pocket, relieved to find the pill bottle still there. As much as she adored her Uncle Mark—maybe not her biological uncle, but the name she'd known him by her whole life—she couldn't shake the notion that he might be concealing something.

"You need to learn how to relax a little," he said, handing her a highball. "You seem a little jumpy, on edge."

She took a drink and grimaced. Uncle Mark poured a strong one.

"Oh, well, yeah," she stammered. "It's weird being back here; Mitch being gone. My car's in the shop. I wanted to leave tomorrow after the will reading, but I'll be stranded here a few more days."

"Car trouble, that bites. But hanging with your sister and those adorable kids of hers has got to be a good trade-off."

"Can't deny that." She took another sip of her drink, and let the liquid run slowly down her throat, warming her from the inside out.

"The last will and testament of the great Mitch Bennett," he began as he took a seat in a high-back across from Carly. He set the bottle next to his glass on the side table. "Funny how a few pieces of paper can cause such an uproar."

"Yeah? What's that mean?" Carly was pleased to know that she might not have to ask awkward, pointed questions. Uncle Mark might just spill some secrets. He'd already downed his drink and was making another.

He was quiet as he poured the whiskey, this time straight, no soda, and didn't start talking again until he'd taken a healthy swig.

"I'm sure you know about Mitch's diagnosis?"

"Well, I know he supposedly died of complications from the virus."

"No, I mean the dementia." He let that word hang in the air while he took another shot of his drink.

"Dementia? No, I hadn't heard. When did this happen?"

"Oh, about a year ago. I'd noticed the old boy wasn't as clearheaded as he used to be. Sharp as a tack back in the day. It's how he became so successful." Uncle Mark spun his glass and stared into it, his face fixed with a contemplative expression that made him appear as if he was expecting guidance from the amber liquid. "But he started repeating things and would get bent out of shape if you pointed it out to him. He was off. Thought nothing of it till Janace said she was trying to get him to a doctor."

"Wow, this is the first I've heard any of this."

"Affected his short-term more than the stuff from a while back. He could tell you the make, model and year of almost any car he drove when he was young, but got to where he couldn't find his own car in the lot when we went out to lunch and such."

"So, what does that have to do with the will?" she pressed.

"He started talking about wanting to change it. Made Janace awful nervous. She didn't want him unloading all his spoils on, say, a new building in his name on campus or something."

"Something like his oldest daughters?"

"Ha! Maybe." He still hadn't taken his eyes off his glass.

Carly took another sip of hers. She was on a roll now and needed to stay ahead of the man, but she knew the drink might give her a little more courage.

"A mistress?" she questioned, and Uncle Mark lost eye contact with his drink.

"Guess that could be," he said, taking his time to form the words as if he were thinking back for any signs he might have missed. He shook his head and took another drink. "Who knows, really? Sometimes you think you know a person inside and out and then they surprise you. But Janace, well, she tried to use his dementia to block any changing of that will this late in the game; not that any of us expected his days to be numbered so few. That woman's done everything in her power to find out what might be in the new one, if there even is a new one. She isn't a hundred percent certain."

"I can see why she'd be flipping out then. Not much she can do to stop it tomorrow, is there?"

"Guess it'll depend on the dates, maybe." He got up and took Carly's glass. Hers wasn't yet empty, but she figured that was for the best and she'd save him a trip. She was relieved to see he had gone to the bar to add soda to hers.

"Enough about all that business." He shuffled back to Carly and gave her the drink. There was a slight tremor in his hand, and he leaned over a touch too far. For a moment, Carly was afraid he'd fall on top of her.

"How are things in, what is it, Tucson?"

"Tempe," she replied.

"Right, Tempe, home of the Sun Devils. Is there a special man in your life?"

"Not unless you count my cat," she laughed.

"Come on now, a gal as pretty as you? You shouldn't be cuddling up to nothing but a cat at night."

"The past couple of years have been hard on us singles."

"Well, that's what online dating is for," he replied.

"No thanks! I'll wait for fate to intervene. You know me and my trust issues." She needed to change the subject to something that might garner her some information. "When you can't trust the two people you should trust the most, it's hard to trust anyone."

"Sure, sure," he began. The Oklahoma drawl he worked hard to suppress was coming through stronger with each sip of his drink. "But you know, sometimes you just gotta let go of all the baggage and take a leap of faith."

"If you say so," she laughed, eager to change topics. She searched her mind for a new path to lead him down. "Speaking of trust. I've always been too afraid to ask this question. Maybe you know the answer. Did Mitch pay for

Mother's funeral? When Liv and I asked about the bill, the people at Strode said it'd been taken care of. The only person I could imagine it could be was Mitch."

"Well, now," he began. "I'd wanted to take this one to the grave, but since you asked. It was me and your Aunt Charlene."

Carly near spit her drink out. "You?"

"And Aunt Charlene, don't forget her. If I recall, she was the one who came up with the idea. Sadly, Mitch never said a word to me about your mother's passing. I was the man's best friend for decades, but never approved of the way he treated you and your sister. I'll kick myself for the rest of my life for not standing up to him and letting him know how badly he failed you and Liv."

Carly studied the man's face. His gaze was lost inside his glass again. She saw a tear slide down his face, and her heart ached. She'd pushed him down this path and regretted it now.

She rose from her seat and slipped her shoes back on before approaching him. She leaned down and gave him a hug. He held her tightly.

She opened her mouth to say something comforting when the energy of the room became electric. It felt as if the heater had been turned on. Every light bulb in the space grew brighter. The television came on, music blaring, the volume so loud that neither of them could hear the other. Actors portraying seizure patients danced around a large of bottle of Keperra on screen. The door to the office slammed open and shut.

Carly released Uncle Mark from the embrace.

"Turn it off," she yelled, her voice unable to match the volume of the television speaker.

A framed photo was hurled by an invisible hand, yanked from its spot on the wall. It fell at Carly's feet. The glass shattered, but she could make out who was in the picture: Uncle

Mark, her father, and Janace. The three stood side by side while Mitch cut a ribbon with oversized scissors.

The door to the office banged open again. Iva stood at the threshold, her mouth agape, clearly shocked by what she was witnessing.

All at once, the commotion ceased. The television snapped off, and the door gently swung closed on Iva.

Carly looked around the office, uncertain of what she was looking for. Until now she could tell herself that the other strange occurrences could be explained away—faulty electric, a person posing as her father, figments of a stressed-out imagination. She could no longer deny that something unworldly was going on. This time there were witnesses.

Chapter Seventeen

2022

After the baffling disturbance in Uncle Mark's office, Carly and Iva cleaned the broken glass and walked Uncle Mark down to one of the rooms. He was snoring before they could turn off the lights and exit.

"What was that?" Iva asked as Carly walked her back to the hotel lobby.

"I wish I knew," Carly replied. "Are you sure you'll be okay up here alone for the rest of the night?"

Iva unlocked the door to the lobby and went about turning on every light, an act Carly understood all too well. Carly went to the back door of the lobby and double-checked it was locked.

"I'll be fine. My brother is on his way up. Said he'd stay with me after I told him, well ... he should be here any minute. Doubt Mr. Watts will have any memory of it. Seems he had a little too much to drink tonight."

"Probably for the best! I'd offer to stay, but I've had a day and tomorrow likely won't be any easier," Carly said, looking at her phone. She groaned. "Ugh, I mean, today won't be any easier. How'd it get so late?"

Car lights spilled across the room and a car door slammed.

"That'd be Marlow. Have a good night, Carly."

"You too. If you need me, please don't hesitate to knock." Carly knocked on the wall.

"Will do."

Back in her room, Carly changed into a T-shirt and shorts, washed her face, and brushed her teeth. All the while, she grappled with the events of the night. She needed to talk to someone about everything—seeing her dead father, getting messages from him, the ridiculous issues with the televisions and the weird commercial. She remembered the bottle she'd secreted in her dress pocket and dug through her dirty clothes pile until she found it.

Taking a closer look, she confirmed that the prescription was for Keperra. She had a hunch who the medication had been prescribed to, and she was right. The drug had been intended for Charlene Watts.

It was well past midnight. She needed to get some sleep. The reading of the will was to take place in less than twelve hours, but she was far too wired to nod off. Opening her phone, she searched for Keperra online. As the commercial indicated, the drug was primarily used for seizures. The fact that the meds were for Aunt Char tracked. So why was the bottle in her father's trash can?

She pulled up the side effects of the drug. It was a lengthy list. Some of the less troublesome were things like drowsiness, dizziness, trouble sleeping, runny nose and sneezing, but the others were downright frightful. Things like neurosis, mistrust, rapidly changing moods, combativeness, anxiety, and delusions of persecution. Reviewing the side effects, she remembered hearing them in the advertisement. Now, the laundry list of issues became more ominous. Was her father taking the medication? Did he suffer from seizures? Having just found out about his dementia diagnosis, it was obvious Janace wouldn't divulge that information to her. If he were taking Keperra, the side effects seemed to mimic some symptoms of dementia.

The prescription hadn't been written for Mitch, though. It was her Aunt Char. Carly felt sorry for her aunt. The medications the poor woman was required to take seemed almost as dreadful as the condition.

Still, the nagging question ran circles in her mind. Was the package that Janace brought to Uncle Mark the same medication? It seemed like a logical assumption given their exchange during the handoff and the fact that a bottle was in Mitch's possession when he died.

She lay in bed and tried to piece together the shreds of information she had. It was no use. She couldn't see through all the noise in her head to come up with any rational explanations. Her eyes grew heavy. She put her phone in the charger on the nightstand and rolled over, pulling the blankets up. No sooner had she drifted off when she heard a notification on her phone. She never would have considered checking the message this late, but concern that it was Iva pushed her to grab the phone.

It wasn't Iva. It was another text from Mitch Bennett.

FATHER: *Talk to Rachel.*

"Rachel?" she questioned out loud to the empty room. She'd hardly shared more than twenty words with Rachel since the woman married her half-brother.

Everything she knew about Rachel she'd learned from Liv. Janace never really accepted the girl, was certain she'd married her son for his money. That fact made her laugh. If it weren't for Mitch, Chip would have nothing, no money, no cars, no dream house, no job.

Rachel had a miscarriage two or three years ago and struggled to conceive again. But now she was expecting, and as far as Carly knew, this pregnancy was going well.

She'd only learned of her former job as a nurse assistant recently, had never really cared to ask before. To say Rachel was shy would be an understatement. Then again, maybe she wasn't shy; maybe she was introverted in the company of the Bennett clan. Carly wouldn't blame the woman.

And exactly what was she supposed to talk to Rachel about? It didn't make sense.

As she pondered it all, she got another ping on her phone. This time a video attachment, again from the person claiming to be her father.

She hoped this wasn't some spoofing attack as she knew not to open unsolicited videos, but there was too much at stake to ignore it.

The video was grainy and in black-and-white. It appeared to be from a surveillance camera set above the scene. Two people walked into view and approached the door of a building. Carly paused the video here and zoomed in to see if she could figure out where the video was taken. There appeared to be an address on the door, but it was too pixelated to decipher. She slowed things down and reviewed the video frame by frame. One of the people reached for the door and when it was drawn back, a logo came into view. Immediately, she recognized the trademark. It was Women's Trust Clinic in Oklahoma City. While the facility aided women in all matters of gynecological health, they were best known for a controversial health service they provided. Women's Trust provided abortions.

Confident she'd pinpointed the location of the cryptic video, she tried to identify the people. Slowly, methodically, she reviewed each frame. The women appeared to be roughly the same height and weight. Carly identified one of the women's purses as designer and expensive. The woman with the familiar bag turned back to look over her shoulder, as if to take in her surroundings or make sure no one saw them. It was Janace. There was no doubt in Carly's mind, despite the low quality of the footage.

Janace, a staunch pro-lifer who rallied people across the state to fight for the cause, at an abortion clinic. The woman had undoubtedly been to the facility before, but she would have been harassing the patients seeking medical attention. She was the one who wielded picket signs with horrible images. She was not the one who held the door open for another woman and willingly entered a clinic that provided abortions.

Carly rolled onto her stomach and played the video from start to finish. The woman with Janace never showed her face. There was no way to tell who it was. She was certain it was not Kimmi. Kimmi had very long and very blonde hair. This person had shoulder-length hair that was darker. The video ended once the two women stepped inside the building. Carly watched it a few more times, and with each viewing, she became more convinced she was right about her stepmother and the building she entered. Her frustration mounted as she attempted to identify the person with Janace. Taking one last look at the playback, she noted the time stamp. The video was taken on the morning of April 17, 2020, just over two years ago. The date held no significance to Carly.

She put the phone back on the nightstand and lay awake, fighting back tears. She needed sleep to clear her head.

"Why me, Mitch?" she whispered.

As she spoke the words, a notification dinged on her phone.

FATHER: *You're the only one I can trust.*

Chapter Eighteen

2022

Carly awoke to the sound of her phone ringing. She blindly groped the nightstand, unwilling to open her eyes until she found the phone. Through one squinted eye, she saw the caller was Liv and slid the green bar.

"Good morning, sunshine," Liv said.

Carly groaned.

"Uh-oh, someone waking up on the wrong side of the bed? Well, cheer up. I have news."

Carly didn't respond to her sister but contemplated hanging up on her so she could go back to sleep.

"What news, you ask, dear sister?" Liv said. "Thank you for asking, Carly. Why, it is news regarding the long-awaited reading of the will."

Carly remained silent, knowing Liv would continue.

"News of the will reading, you say? Yes, of monumental importance as well. You see, darling sister, the reading of the will has been canceled today."

Liv allowed for a long pause before continuing.

"Hello, is this thing on? Are you still there? Did you hear what I said?"

Carly finally caved. "Yes, I'm here. I heard you."

"So that begs the question: whatever could delay the reading of the recently deceased patriarch's will?"

"Yep, whatever could delay the—" Carly trailed off.

"Janace is sick. That's it. The entire family can just wait another day or two because Janace is sick. And what might she be sick with, you might inquire. The virus. The same fake news, 5G plandemic illness that most of us have been vaccinated for by now. Of course, she wasn't vaccinated because she wasn't going to allow the government to inject a chip into her body that could track her every move, as if her phone hadn't been doing that for years. Of course, it might be allergies. The whole thing is off pending her test results. Can you believe her?"

"Did you really just ask if I can believe that Janace might try to hinder the reading of the will?" Carly asked, knowing she'd only fuel her sister's fire.

"Well, okay, you got me there, but has she not heard of video conferencing? So we will wait. But while we wait, we should do so with waffles! I'm coming to get you. We're going to Just Wafflin'. Derek's parents have the kids. I'm free for the day."

"You had me at waffles. There's a lot I need to talk to you about. Give me thirty minutes."

"Yay!" Liv exclaimed. "See you soon!"

————

With the promise of a Nutty Fosters waffle, Carly scanned the available seats at Just Wafflin'. She spotted a seat for two at the back of the restaurant and made a beeline to the table. She wanted something secluded so she could unload all the things that had been tying her in knots since her arrival in Stillwater.

"Why'd you pick the table closest to the bathroom?" Liv complained as she sat down.

"The things I need to talk to you about are kind of…" Carly searched for the word. "Sensitive."

"Oh, my favorite! Sensitive topics over waffles. This ought to be good! Spill!"

Carly wasn't sure where to start. While she'd mulled over the idea of divulging things to her sister, she had given little thought to what to say and how to say it.

"So, things got weird on my way out here," Carly started.

Her sister held her cappuccino to her lips. Steam rose from the mug and she blew gently on the drink, never taking her eyes off of Carly.

"My radio started acting up."

As soon as the words escaped her, she saw the look of utter disappointment on Liv's face. Maybe she shouldn't have started with the most benign occurrence.

A waitress approached and placed their plates on the table. She also set the syrup carrier down and pointed out the specialty flavors. Liv grabbed the cinnamon sauce and began drizzling it over her Peachy Keen waffles. As soon as the waitress left, she started in on Carly.

"We had to sit by the bathrooms so you could tell me about your car troubles?" Liv complained, her eyes now fixed on her plate. "I mean, yeah, that sucks, but I was expecting something a bit more juicy."

"Trust me, it gets weirder." She decided to skip over the problems with the stereo. "I started getting text messages from Mitch."

Liv set her fork down and stared at Carly. Carly could tell she wanted to speak, but her mouth was full of gooey peaches in cinnamon sauce. Carly pushed on since her sister was rendered speechless.

"He also started following me on my socials … He comments on my pictures. Likes all of my posts."

Liv grabbed her drink and washed her food down.

"So, like before he died? Who knows, maybe he was beyond bored lying in bed sick. I mean, I get it and I'm trying not to be offended by him only hitting you up on socials, but maybe he just didn't get to me yet before things got dire for him. It's kind of nice, really. A sign that maybe on some level he actually cared?"

"No, Liv. None of this happened while he was alive. The messages, the feedback on my socials, all of it happened after he was dead."

"Okay, you know that sounds ridiculous, right? I mean, yes, it's strange, but the strangest part is, who would pull something like that on you? It's cruel."

"I agree, harsh. Of course, I believed it to be a prank as well," Carly replied. She hadn't yet touched her waffles and grabbed the syrup, drizzling it over the waffles before taking a bite.

"Proceed," Liv said.

"Oh, the night you called me, when you told me about Father's death, I was having a dream about him. It was like I knew he was dead before you even called."

"Well, you have had some premonition-y things happen to you. Remember the time I was in the car accident and your back started hurting the minute I was injured? You knew. Or the time you dreamed about your roommate ... what was her name, Susan?"

"Sarah."

"Yeah, right, Sarah."

Carly remembered the incident. She'd had a dream her roommate showed up with an infant. In the dream, Sarah asked Carly to help her with the baby, but Carly refused. The dream nagged her the next day. She would never refuse to help a close friend with a newborn. She loved babies. Later that evening, Sarah came home sobbing. She'd had an abortion. While she hadn't told anyone about it before, she could no longer keep it to herself once the procedure was done. Carly felt horrible for Sarah but believed that was the answer to her questions about her dream. There was no baby for Carly to help with anymore.

"You had that dream," Liv said before cramming a bite into her mouth.

"Yeah, I know. Maybe, but there's more. I've seen him, Liv. I've seen Mitch."

Liv dropped her fork. A few patrons glanced their way as the fork clattered to the floor. Liv let it remain on the floor and seemed to have forgotten about her unfinished waffles.

"Carly, come on. It's one thing to have portentous dreams, but seeing what ... a ghost? I mean, don't get me wrong. I love a good ghost story as much as the next person, but—"

"Liv, I need you to stick with me here and have an open mind."

"Okay, okay, let me grab a new fork." Liv rushed to the beverage station and hurried back. She held two forks. "Just in case," she shrugged. "So, these Mitch sightings, where were they? Did you talk to him?"

"He doesn't talk. He texts."

"Right, right. Can you show me these texts?"

"Yes!" Carly exclaimed. As she rummaged through her purse for the phone, dread gripped her. What if the messages weren't really there? She found the phone and scrolled through her text messages. There they were, the ones from Mitch. She heaved a sigh of relief and handed her phone to Liv.

Liv perused the messages and passed the phone back to Carly.

"You're right. Weird. Nevertheless, I think you should focus on finding out who is sending these and back away from the seeing-your-dead-father narrative."

"Liv, come on. You think I'm losing my mind or something? I'm not making any of this up."

"No, not losing your mind, but there's a lot of stress surrounding all of this. It would be perfectly understandable if you were processing his passing in a not-so-typical fashion."

"He wants my help, Liv."

"Your help? Sure, the texts are cryptic, but how are you supposed to help a dead person? Seems like he's pretty much beyond helping at this point."

"I don't know how I'm supposed to help him. I forgot to tell you I saw Janace at the motel with Uncle Mark. She handed him a package and told him he could return it to Charlene. She kissed him too. I mean, it wasn't a passionate kiss; more like the way you'd kiss a friend, but still weird. Oh, my gosh, did you know about Mitch's dementia?" Carly was overwhelmed with the information she'd withheld from her sister. There was no clear path to take. No way to make sense of it.

"Wait, what? He had dementia? Who told you that?" Liv reached for her coffee cup, a pout twisting on her face as she realized it was empty. She sat the cup on the table. "I have a million questions right now. All of them are what the hell are you talking about?"

"I get it and I'm sorry. Uncle Mark told me about Father's diagnosis. But here's the crazy part—"

"It gets crazier than what you've told me so far? I'm not sure I can take any more."

"So, the televisions at the motel are possessed. They just turn off and on at random and the things on the screens are super weird."

"Didn't I just ask you to tone down the cuckoo?" Liv pushed her plate away, her waffle only half-eaten.

"At first it was some old movie," Carly pressed on. "It looked familiar, but I'm not sure what it was. The TV would turn on by itself, volume up all the way. After a few times, it wasn't a movie anymore, it was a commercial."

"Carly, I'm seriously having a hard time absorbing all this."

"I know, it's a lot. I should have told you sooner, but it's taken me time to process all of it. The television ad is for a prescription medicine called Keppera. It's for people who have seizures. Last night I saw Mitch at his house."

Carly saw the disbelief flash in Liv's eyes. "Carls—"

"Liv, he was there. I followed him down the hall to his bedroom."

"You went into Janace's bedroom?"

"Yes, I wasn't thinking. I was just following. He spilled over the trash can."

"You not only went into Janace's room, but you vandalized it as well?"

"I didn't knock it over," Carly insisted.

The complexities of the conversation were overwhelming. Carly felt nauseous; her palms were clammy. She'd been twisting her napkin into knots. Now she tore away tiny bits of it, forming a pile of shredded paper. "A pill bottle rolled out of the overturned trash can. A pill bottle for Keppera. But Mitch's name wasn't on the prescription. It was Charlene's medication."

"Wait, so you think the package Janace gave to Uncle Mark was the pill bottle?"

"Yes!"

"And if I may be so bold, you think Janace was giving Aunt Char's medicine to Mitch?"

"That's right!" Carly sat up straight, queasiness forgotten. She was relieved that Liv was jumping to the same conclusions as her.

"But why would Janace give Charlene's pills to Mitch?"

"I haven't figured that out exactly, but I have a hunch. I don't know if I should tell you. It's pretty far-fetched."

Liv rolled her eyes. "I've stayed with you up to this point. I can count on one finger the number of things you've told me this morning that weren't far-fetched. Not to mention, you've totally killed the waffle vibe."

"What if Mitch didn't have dementia? What if Janace gave him the pills to make it look like he was losing his grip?"

Carly paused and let Liv absorb what she'd said. She could see Liv's mind at work processing the info dump. After a couple of minutes, Liv spoke.

"Do you think Mitch died of an overdose? Do you think Janace"—Liv leaned in close to Carly, her eyes darting back and forth, and whispered—"killed him?"

"Oh, wow! I hadn't even thought of that. That seems a bit extra."

"Extra? Really? After everything you've said here, I'm the one making a bizarre story even more fantastic?" Liv's voice was close to full volume now. Only a few tables remained occupied in the dining room. Several patrons glanced at Liv and Carly. "So tell me, what do you think the reason would be for her to give her husband a medication that didn't belong to him?"

"Well, the side effects for Keperra are pretty intense, and they mimic the symptoms of someone experiencing dementia."

"So she gave Mitch something to make him seem like he was losing his faculties? But why? What would her motive be?"

"I have my suspicions."

"You going to share these suspicions, or do I have to guess?"

"What if she was using the drug to alter Mitch's state of mind so she could contest any new directives he made?"

"Directives?"

"Like the will. When did you say he called to ask about what we should get when he dies? A couple of years ago, right?"

"I think that's right."

"Uncle Mark said Mitch's long-term memory was intact. It was the short-term that he had problems with." Carly waited to see that Liv was still with her. Liv nodded her head.

"Here's where that theory falls apart, in my opinion," Liv said. "If Mitch was going to add us to his will, and that's a big if, I can't believe that he was going to do something drastic like leave his entire estate to you and me. In reality, if we do get anything, I fully expect it to be paltry. No stake in his businesses; those are run by Chip, Kimmi and Lance. He wouldn't give us a house; his extra acreage already houses his two favored children. I just can't see him willing us anything that would compel Janace to take such extreme measures."

Carly concentrated on each word. Liv was right. Drugging her husband would be too risky to prevent her stepchildren from receiving a few hundred thousand dollars. The man was worth much more.

"There's more to the story," Carly said.

"Carly, I don't think I can take much more. This is all way too much to take in without caffeine, and my mug is empty. Let's go grab the tallest cup at Aspen Coffee, and you can tell me the rest."

———

The sisters were silent as they made their way to the coffeehouse. Their conversation didn't resume until they'd ordered their drinks and settled into a couch tucked into a quiet corner.

"Where do you go from here with all of this?" Liv asked.

"I'm not sure, but there's more."

"But of course," Liv retorted.

"I've been told to talk to Rachel."

"Rachel? Mousy, little pretend-you-don't-see-me Rachel? What could she possibly have to add to this?"

"I'm not sure. Maybe her medical knowledge? Maybe she

heard something. I haven't got a clue. But last night, Mitch sent me a video clip."

"Our dead father is sending you TikToks? This should be rich."

"Carly and Liv," the barista called from behind the counter.

"Stay put. I'll grab them," Carly said, getting up from the couch.

When she returned, Liv was looking at her phone.

"We're going to have to take those drinks to go," she told Carly as she approached.

"Is everything okay with the kids?" Carly asked.

"Yes, they're fine. But someone has just been admitted to the hospital."

"Who? Janace? Don't tell me she's actually really sick?"

"Nope, not Janace. None other than mousy, pretend-you-don't-see-me Rachel." Liv grabbed her purse and headed for the door.

Chapter Nineteen

2022

While driving to the hospital, Carly questioned Liv.

"Tell me again why we're going to the hospital," Carly said.

"To see Rachel. Really Carly, keep up." Liv tapped the steering wheel nervously, chewing on her lip as she waited for the light to turn green.

"And Rachel would want us to visit her in the hospital why?"

"Ugh, Carly, do I have to explain everything?" Liv said, smashing the gas pedal.

"Yes, you do."

"Fine! We aren't going to see Rachel in the hospital," Liv replied.

"Oh, so we're not going to the hospital?"

Liv took her eyes off the road and fixed Carly with a look of complete disbelief. "Yes, we are going to the hospital. But we can't make it look like we know about Rachel."

"Who told you she was in the hospital?"

"A certain someone who could get in worlds of trouble if

said someone were to share confidential patient information with me."

"Oh, so Derek," Carly said.

"No, not Derek. Derek is not the person. Let's just say a little birdie."

"A little birdie with a medical degree then," Carly said, just to push her sister's buttons.

Liv parked in the physician's parking lot. "One of the perks of being married to a birdie with a medical degree," she said.

The two exited the car, and Liv laid out a plan as they crossed the parking lot.

"So we just came to see my husband," she started.

"Why did we come to see your husband?" Carly asked.

"Right, we need a reason. Give me your coffee," Liv said, taking Carly's cup from her. "We were close by and decided to bring him a caffeinated pick-me-up."

Carly relinquished the beverage willingly. She was exhausted, hadn't slept well one night since arriving, but knew she didn't need more caffeine. She was already on edge.

"We are bringing Derek coffee, and we just happen to what? Wait, I haven't thought that far ahead. It's not like she'll be cruising the halls or in the cafeteria line. Shoot! How do we accidentally run into her on purpose?"

"Got me," Carly replied as the automatic doors swooshed open and they entered.

"Oh, I don't know. We'll just have to play it by ear. But whatever happens, Derek is not the little birdie!"

"Got it."

The two got on the elevator and rode in silence. An elderly couple rode with them. Liv smiled and nodded as she leaned forward to hit the button for the second floor.

As Liv and Carly exited the elevator, they bumped into Derek.

"Hey, sweetheart, look what I brought you," Liv cooed, handing the cup to her husband.

"Wow, to what do you owe this pleasure?" Derek said with the smoothness of a pimply-faced preteen boy speaking to the prettiest girl in class. He took a swig of the coffee and grimaced. "Oh, wow, just how I like it, lukewarm."

"Correction, lukewarm with backwash," Carly interjected.

"It's the thought that counts," Liv replied.

"You two follow me," he said.

Derek ducked behind a temporary wall. This part of the hospital was under construction.

"I told you not to say anything to anyone," Derek whispered between clenched teeth; a false smile strained his face.

"Carly's not anyone, honey," Liv replied, mimicking her husband's expression.

"Guys, I'm right here. I can hear you." Carly said.

"Listen, I was trying to get some information for you, but you can't just walk in here and expect me to escort you to her room."

"We don't need an escort, just a room number," Liv said.

"You know how much I hate telling you no, but no. I should've kept my mouth shut."

"Don't be silly," Liv said. "You've got the resourcefulness of the Bennett sisters here. We'll figure something out."

"Figure it out without me," Derek replied as his beeper went off. He checked the small device. "Look, I've got to go. I'm being paged. Please, just let this pass. Go on about your day. Thanks for the coffee, I think." He gave his wife a peck on the cheek.

"Don't you worry about us," Liv said, sweetly.

Carly and Liv watched Derek disappear around a corner as they emerged from behind the construction divider. They moved slowly toward the elevator bank. Carly wished Liv would take her husband's advice and leave. She knew better. An elevator door opened, and Janace stepped off.

Liv grabbed Carly's elbow and dug her nails in.

"Ouch!"

"Shhh! Look who it is! We'll follow. Act cool."

"Cool, right, just like we've been this whole time. I don't know, Liv."

"Hush, Carly, this is fate. Don't lose her."

Janace moved through the maze of the hospital floor, stopping to read room numbers when faced with a turn. Liv and Carly stayed ten feet back, even pretending to blend in with other groups of visitors so as not to stand out.

"Good thing we're on the most secure floor of the entire facility," Carly whispered. "We probably look like we're here to swipe a baby."

Janace stopped at a closed door and knocked. Liv and Carly were too far back to hear the exchange, but Janace opened the door and entered the room.

Liv turned to Carly, eyes wide. "How'd we get so lucky?"

"I don't call this luck. I call it stupidity."

Liv grabbed Carly's hand and dragged her down the hall. Janace had not closed the door all the way. Liv leaned against the wall near the door and pulled her phone out, pretending to be checking something important; Carly followed suit.

"We look so suspicious," Carly whispered.

"No, we don't. We're here visiting our sister-in-law, and she's getting a sponge bath or something. We politely stepped into the hall to give her privacy."

Liv moved closer to the door and Carly inched closer to her sister. Janace greeted Rachel. Carly could hear the pregnant woman sobbing.

"What is going on? Why did they admit you?" Janace questioned.

Through gasping breaths, Rachel replied, "I thought I was having contractions. Maybe I overreacted."

"Of course you overreacted. You should have just called me and I could have come over."

"I thought you were sick. Chip said—"

"I'm fine. It's just allergies."

"I shouldn't have to stay much longer. Just until the non-stress test is done. The little guy is kicking up a storm now, and the doctor said all was well with me. I just can't lose this pregnancy too."

"Last time you didn't lose the baby. We made a decision about ending that pregnancy, and it was the right decision."

"No, it was most definitely not the right decision, Janace. I've never recovered. I think about what could have been all the time." Rachel was sobbing again.

In the hallway, Carly had forgotten about trying not to look sketchy. She thought back to the video, and it hit her. She did know the person Janace escorted into the clinic. It was Rachel.

"Snap out of it! I'm letting you have this baby. Once he's born, you'll forget all about the other."

"No! I won't forget," Rachel said, raising her voice. "That baby should have lived. I never should have let you talk me into terminating it."

Now Liv had given up on pretend phone scrolling too. She looked at Carly, eyes wide, and mouthed the word, *"Abortion?"*

"You told me to get pregnant. You said it could be with anyone. I would have never told Chip the baby wasn't his."

"Well, when I said to get knocked up by anyone, I meant anyone but Kimmi's husband!"

On the other side of the door, Liv grabbed Carly's arm and squeezed.

"I should have never told you who the father of the baby was. I don't know why I let you pressure me into divulging that information. If I'd just kept my mouth shut, I would have that baby in my arms right now. I'll never forgive myself." Rachel spoke through her sobs.

"Can you imagine how that would look? Not to mention the fact that Chip is blond and Lance has dark hair. The two look nothing alike. If you hadn't told me, I would have known the minute that baby popped out. And then it would have been too late. Besides, how horrid would it look if someone found out? Kimmi's kids would be siblings to your baby. They'd be cousins and siblings, Rachel. That pregnancy never should have happened. It was an abomination!"

"She was not an abomination!" Rachel yelled. The bitterness rang clear, even outside the room. "It was bad enough you let me try for over two years knowing your son couldn't even get me pregnant! It's sadistic, Janace! You're heartless!"

"I'm heartless?" Janace boomed. "I allowed you to get pregnant by my own husband! How is that heartless? It was the perfect solution. Having your brother-in-law's baby ... I would never allow anyone to muddy the waters that way! The child wouldn't possess a drop of Bennett blood. This, this child you are carrying, is a true Bennett. You need to settle down, or you're going to put this pregnancy in jeopardy!"

Outside the hospital room, Carly clamped her hand over her mouth, not only to keep her from gasping out loud, but to prevent her from being sick. She wanted to run. Now she grabbed Liv's hand and pulled her away from the door.

"Stop, I want to hear this," Liv protested.

"I can't! I can't listen to any more of this. I think we've learned way too much already. I want to get out of here." Carly did not let up, despite Liv digging in.

"Fine," Liv said. "Let go of me."

Carly released her grip, and Liv followed her to the elevator. The doors slid open, and Carly was glad to see they would be alone. Once inside, she bent over, placing her hands on her knees. Wave after wave of nausea hit her. She wasn't sure she'd be able to hold the waffles down.

The two half-walked, half-jogged to the car. Liv started the engine and turned the air conditioner on full blast.

"Oh, my God, Carly," Liv said. "What did we just hear?

That can't be true! They told everyone she miscarried. I made like four casseroles for her."

"That's your takeaway? She slept with Mitch! The child she is carrying is our half-brother. And our nephew." Carly grimaced. The words left a foul taste in her mouth.

"Stop talking! I can't get the image out of my head! What on earth? It's sickening, Carls!"

"That's one word that comes to mind. I feel like I need a shower. We should get out of here. I don't want Janace to see us. Ugh, how will I ever look at either of them again?"

Liv pulled out of the parking lot.

"I hate to abandon you, but I need to lie down. You mind taking me back to the Roadside?"

"I'm with you. Might need to rest a spell myself."

Carly and Liv pulled into the parking lot of the Roadside Motel. Uncle Mark was backing his truck out of a spot in front of the lobby. From inside his truck, he tipped his hat, and Carly held her breath. There was no way she could carry on a normal conversation. Fortunately, he drove to the exit and turned onto the highway.

Carly and Liv hurried into the room and dropped onto the beds.

"Why are there two unmade beds in here?" Liv asked.

"If I told you, you wouldn't believe me," Carly replied.

"I don't think I'll ever be able to believe anything again. I can't bring myself to accept what we just heard is real. It's like the universe just went into a tailspin."

"You have to believe at least some of what I told you. Mitch said I needed to talk to Rachel and, well, I didn't actually talk to her, but I'm pretty sure that is the information he wants me to know."

"We need another name for your mystery texter. Mitch is just too, I don't know, much. Just too much."

"Call him whatever you want, but I can't ignore the things I've been experiencing."

Liv sighed and sat up. "I think I need to go hold my babies. It's the only thing I can think of doing that might make me feel better."

"You're such a wonderful mom, Liv. I don't know how you do it. Where did you find the skills needed to be so good at it? You were certainly never shown."

"I don't know. I think Mother loved us. In her own way."

"I'm sorry, but the only thing she loved more than herself was booze and pills."

"It's okay to let up on it, you know. Forgive her, move on. It really helps. I don't think I would have allowed myself to get married and have my own kids if I clung—" Liv stopped herself.

"Forgot who you were talking to there, huh?"

"I'm sorry, Carls, but it kind of proves my point. That life, we were given that life. This is the life I've made. It's a good life."

"You always were her favorite anyway," Carly mumbled.

"And you were always too hard on her." Liv said.

"Too hard? On her? Liv, she wasted her life in pills. She was too wrapped up in fulfilling her own needs to strive for a better life for her children. Think how much easier life would have been if it had been bankrolled by our father. She could've taken Mitch to court, asked for more child support so we didn't live off of free school meals and food stamps. She didn't do that. She'd rather us wallow in her addiction than help us out."

"Carly, she was up against more than just her own demons. She didn't want to rely on Father, because that meant she actually relied on Janace. It was humiliating for her."

"Oh, poor Catherine. The helpless, innocent victim of her own poor decisions." Carly got up from the bed and went to the window, pulling back the heavy curtain. Sunshine breathed new life into the room, but not into Carly. Her sister was right. Carly hadn't been able to forgive their mother, and the anger was unrelenting.

"Did you know what Janace sent when you and I turned eighteen?"

"No clue," Carly responded, flopping down in the desk chair. "A birthday card with a twenty?"

"She calculated the number of days in the month we turned eighteen; fourteen days for you and twenty-three for me."

"I don't get it."

"The child support. She figured out what the per diem was for the paltry amount Mitch was required to pay. Then she doled out the daily amount times the days in the month that we were seventeen. Refused to pay the full amount from the instant we turned eighteen. Who does that?"

Carly looked at her sister, her expression vapid as she absorbed the words Liv said.

"Mother didn't even want to cash those checks; wanted nothing more than to send them back to Janace. That wasn't an option for her. She needed the money. If there is anyone more repressed by their relationship with Mitch Bennett than you or me, it was her. He took her power. He took her confidence."

"My views on this couldn't differ more from yours. She allowed herself to be swallowed up by the man. Gave up her art, gave up on everything."

"I was in the car with her when she deposited my last child support check. The personalized checks with those cheery Precious Moments images and her perfect handwriting. Mother cried while she filled out the deposit slip. Right there, in the drive-up window to Stillwater National Bank, she sat and sobbed. What was chump change for Janace was lifeblood for Mother."

"Guess we can agree we got a raw deal in the parenting

department. I'm happy you've done better for your kids. I'm not sure I have the fortitude you do."

"Nonsense, Carls." Liv sat up and grabbed Carly's hands. "You'll be a great wife, and an even better mother, if that's what you want. You just have to believe in yourself."

"That's not as easy as it sounds."

"I know. But I believe in you."

"Thank you. But seriously, now we have this whole half-brother from our sister-in-law debacle. Any man with half a brain would run from this microcosm of complete dysfunction. You're lucky you snared Derek before this bombshell dropped."

"It's definitely not first-date material," Liv laughed. "I'm gonna go hug those babies now. You'll be all right?"

"Yep."

Liv hugged her sister. "I'm making dinner for the in-laws tonight. I can send Derek by to pick you up later if you want to join us."

"Nah, pretty sure I'm not fit for company, at least not of the familial type. I'll order pizza or something. Maybe share it with Iva."

"Oh, yeah. I haven't met her. But her story might rival even ours. Well, ours before today. But that's a whole other can of worms. We've got plenty of creepy crawlers to tend to ourselves right now. Rest up, big day tomorrow. Love you a million."

"A million billion," Carly replied.

Chapter Twenty

2022

Carly paced the room, trying to make sense out of all she'd learned. How could Rachel have slept with their father? It was beyond revolting.

She took her phone out and watched the video again. With everything that had happened, she hadn't shown Liv the footage. She wasn't sure it would have helped convince her sister that the things she was experiencing were true. The woman with Janace had to be Rachel. The more times she watched the video, the more she was convinced.

Janace's hypocrisy was mind-blowing. A woman who fought to strip the rights of a woman to end an unwanted pregnancy had the audacity to force Rachel into aborting her child. Ironically, Janace and those with her beliefs were winning the battle; a battle Carly believed had ended in the seventies. The direction things were going, had the abortion been needed now, Janace would not have been able to force Rachel's hand. She'd have faced criminal charges if she'd tried. It was enough to make Carly's head spin.

She scrolled through the messages she'd received from

Mitch and an idea occurred to her, one she couldn't believe she hadn't thought of yet. What would happen if she replied to these messages, or better yet, called the number of the person who sent them?

On her Facebook page, she found the first picture Mitch had commented on. She was relieved to see the comment was still there and took a screenshot to prove to Liv that the comments came after Mitch died. The picture was taken a few years ago. She and her colleagues at the ad agency won an award for a campaign they developed. She couldn't remember who the client was. Dressed in formal attire, Carly stood in the middle of the group holding the trophy. Mitch wrote *Congratulations! What an honor. Wish I'd seen your work.*

A sardonic smile broke on her face. "As if," she said.

It took her a moment to come up with her reply. *All you had to do was call me now and then.* She stared at the words for some time, wishing she could think of a better comeback. In frustration, she hit the reply button. The response was instant. *You're right.*

"Well, at least the man can admit a mistake."

Her finger hovered over the call button, but she couldn't make the move. She tried to reason with herself. *It's just a phone call. He can't hurt me with a phone call.* No matter what logic told her, she hesitated. Annoyed with herself, she took a shower, believing it would clear her head and calm her down.

While the hot water felt good to her body, it did little to assuage her mind. She stood under the hot water far longer than necessary. The tiny bathroom was filled with steam when she stepped out of the shower. She wrapped her body in a towel and stepped to the mirror after cracking the door. As the steam evaporated, letters appeared like phantom scrawls in the mirror. She gasped and yanked the towel off, using it to wipe the bathroom mirror. There was only one word, *MURDER*, stenciled onto the surface in all caps. She draped the towel back over herself and quickly left the bathroom.

She'd forgotten to close the curtains before undressing and screamed as she saw the same word was written on the window. Red dirt mud used to pen the word *murder*. She ran across the room and pulled the curtains. The absence of light rendered the room dusky despite all the lamps being turned on.

She considered ringing Iva or banging on the wall to alert the girl of trouble, but didn't. Instead, she rummaged through her suitcase, pulled out clean shorts and a T-shirt, and dressed. It would be difficult explaining how the word *murder* was scrawled on the window. But maybe there was a camera. Something to show who wrote the frightening message.

Slowly, she approached the window and, with her eyes squeezed shut, she pulled back the curtain a couple of inches. When she opened her eyes, the word was gone. The window was pristine, as if it had just been washed. On some level, she was relieved she wouldn't have to ask Iva for cleaning supplies. She probably shouldn't ask for security footage either.

She grabbed her phone, intending to call Liv, thinking that her sister's voice could calm her. Instead of dialing Liv's number, she called the number that sent the texts claiming to be her father. As the phone rang, she forced herself not to hang up. After the third ring, there was a click followed by loud static, and then the person on the other end of the line spoke.

"Carly, I was murdered."

The phone fell from her grasp and the room flip-flopped. She shrunk onto the bed. There was no denying the voice was her father's.

With no idea how much time had passed, Carly blindly reached for her phone. Her hand recoiled when her fingers brushed against it, but she forced herself to pick it up. What was a source of terror moments ago was now her only hope for deliverance from the fear that gripped her. She called Liv.

"Hey, how are you doing?" Her sister's cheery voice

calmed her instantly. In the background she heard pots banging, Asa crying, and Fallon singing a song about a shark. There was so much warmth and comfort in Liv's surroundings. Carly envied her sister.

"I, um," Carly stammered. The only words she could muster were, "No, not so hot."

"Oh, jeez, I know, right? My mind is a jumble. If it weren't for my in-laws taking care of things, I don't know how I would handle it."

"Liv, I talked to him."

"Talked to who?"

"Mitch, our father. I called the number where the texts have come from. It was him—"

"I'm going to stop you right there. You need to back away from the Mitch stuff, Carls. I'm starting to worry about you."

"No, Liv. It was him. He said he was murdered."

"Murdered? Okay, Carls, sweetie, that's enough. Someone is messing with you—"

Now Carly cut Liv off. "It was him, I swear. I'd recognize the voice anywhere."

"Listen." Liv lowered her voice and Carly could tell her sister had stepped away from the chaos. "Mitch is dead, Carly. We are going to his lawyer's office tomorrow for the will reading. I'm not sure who is doing this to you or why, but it isn't our father reaching out from the grave. People can do wonders with voice generation these days. Maybe it's time we contact the police. Mitch died. He was sick, and he refused to seek medical care. End of story."

"It had to have been Janace. She had to be the one to kill him. Why else would she have him cremated? Oh my God, Liv, there's no way to prove she did it. His body was the only evidence, and it's been incinerated."

"Carly, stop! Hold on a minute. I'm checking Life360 to see if Derek has left the hospital yet. I'm sending him to come pick you up."

"No, Liv—" It was too late. Liv had put her on hold.

Carly paced the room. She went to the window and pulled back the curtain. The sky was darkening under thick gray clouds. Strong winds stirred, blowing pieces of litter, leaves and dust across the parking lot. In the distance, headlights flashed and disappeared on the highway. Carly wished she was in her car, driving away from this place. She wanted nothing more than to be back in Tempe.

"Carly, are you there?" Liv's voice came back. She sounded frantic. "Okay, listen. Someone added Mitch to my Life360."

Carly sat in the room's only chair. "That's weird—"

"Stop talking. That's not the weird part. This app is telling me that Mitch is at the Roadside."

"What?"

"Look out your window. Are there any cars? I don't want you to confront whoever this is, but this could be our chance to figure out who has been messing with you, and now me. How could someone hack my Life360? Why would someone hack my Life360?"

Carly reached for the curtain with a shaky hand. She allowed one eye to peer out into the gloominess of the pop-up storm.

"I see Iva's car, and it looks like Uncle Mark is here. I think that's his truck," Carly reported.

"You don't think—"

"Think what?"

"Uncle Mark?"

"No, not Uncle Mark." Carly shook her head, willing herself to believe the words she said. "He wouldn't do this to me. Would he?"

"Before today, I never would have believed that Rachel would be pregnant with Mitch's baby, nor that Janace, of all people, would force an abortion on a family member."

While Carly searched for words, the call dropped.

"Liv? Are you still there? Can you hear me?" Just as she gave up on the call, a voice erupted on the line.

"Murder!"

She let the phone fall to the floor. The air buzzed with a fiery electric hum. Fine hairs on her arms raised in a hot wave, only to wither in the heat that rolled across the room. The light bulb in the table lamp brightened before snapping in a loud pop that sent shards of thin glass hurling through the air. The overhead light went dark, casting the room into an inky and unfamiliar space.

The television snapped on, and angry static screamed from the speaker. The screen shifted, and the video of Janace and Rachel entering the abortion clinic appeared.

"What do you want from me?" Carly screamed. "If this is you, Mitch, I owe you nothing! You don't have the right to ask for my help!"

Hot tears streamed down her face. From where she stood, she whipped her head around, searching the darkness for something or someone to make the madness stop.

On the television, the video faded before crimson letters appeared in the static. *Murder.*

Carly grabbed her phone and ran for the door. She fled to the hotel lobby and collapsed on the old sofa that offered travelers a place to rest while they perused the local event brochures scattered on the coffee table.

Iva looked up from her computer screen.

"Oh, hey, you having a party next door or what? Things sounded pretty loud. I mean, as long as the room's not trashed, it's no biggie. Not like there are any other guests to disturb."

Carly worked to catch her breath.

"Is Uncle Mark here?" she asked Iva.

"Ah, no, you just missed him."

The news that Uncle Mark had left was good. She

couldn't face the man right now with the suspicions swimming through her mind.

"You want to share a pizza? It's on me," Carly said.

"Oh, wow. That'd be great. Thanks!"

Carly ordered pizza and fried mushrooms from The Hideaway. She texted Liv while she waited for the delivery.

CARLY: *Wanted you to know I am OK. I'm beat. See you tomorrow. Gotta bum a ride to the big event.*

Liv responded in seconds.

LIV: *OMG, thank goodness you are OK. The call dropped and wouldn't go through after that. Derek got held up at the hospital. I've been so worried. If you're sure you're OK, I'll let you rest. See you tomorrow. XO.*

Carly ordered more food than they could eat in one sitting on purpose and insisted Iva and Marlow save the leftovers for themselves.

"Mind if I hang out for a while?" she asked after storing the food in the apartment fridge. "I really don't want to be alone right now."

"Sure thing," Iva replied. "I lock the lobby door at eleven o'clock, but you're welcome to stay as long as you like. Want me to turn the TV on?"

"No, please don't. The quiet is nice."

Chapter Twenty-One

2022

Carly awoke to a sunbeam targeting her face and the sound of a coffee maker percolating. She rubbed her eyes, then shielded them from the sun before taking in her environment. Realizing she was sleeping in the lobby of the Roadside, she bolted up, kicking off a blanket that lay on top of her.

"Morning," Marlow said as he walked through the lobby. He paused at the door. "Let me know if you need anything in your room. I'll be around all day."

"Oh, hey," Carly replied, her face flushed with embarrassment. "There was a little situation in my room last night. A power surge or something. I think a lightbulb or two may have popped."

"Weird. I'll check it out and freshen your towels and bedding."

"There's been a lot of weird around here lately," Iva said from behind the desk.

"We know a thing or two about weird, don't we, Iva?"

"Understatement of the day, Mar," Iva replied.

Carly glanced at the ancient sunburst clock and was

shocked to see that she'd slept in so late. It was almost ten o'clock. Despite crashing out on the ancient, squeaky sofa, she'd slept better than she had in days.

"Oh, wow, the time. I have someplace to be soon. I'll need to shower. How about I take down the *Do Not Disturb* sign when I leave?"

"Sounds like a plan. Have a good one," Marlow replied before leaving.

Carly got up and folded the blanket.

"I hope you don't mind that I didn't wake you last night. You were really wiped out," Iva said as she poured herself a cup of coffee.

"No, not at all. I slept great. I'm the one who should be sorry. Gotta run," she said, walking toward the door.

"No worries. Here," Iva said, handing Carly a cup of coffee. "Looks like you could use this."

"You have no idea," she replied, taking the coffee and making her way to the exit. Before bolting through the door, she thanked Iva.

Carly's hand hovered over the doorknob to her room, afraid to touch it. She wasn't sure what she might find inside, but time was a factor, so she closed her eyes, turned the knob, and pushed the door open. Aside from the unmade beds and some glass on the nightstand, the room was not necessarily pristine, but clean enough.

She hung the *Do Not Disturb* tag on the door and unplugged her phone charger from the bedside, taking it to the bathroom, where she plugged it in and connected her phone before getting ready. She was shocked Liv hadn't given her a wake-up call and decided to make sure the meeting with Mitch's lawyer was still a go.

CARLY: *Green light for will reading?*
Liv responded quickly.
LIV: *Seems as if. I'll pick you up in an hour. We can grab a coffee first.*

CARLY: *Sounds good.*

She opted not to shower and was ready to go with minutes to spare before Liv showed up. Liv beeped her horn and Carly ran out to meet her, remembering at the last minute to toss the *Do Not Disturb* notice back inside the room.

"Are you ready for this?" Liv asked the moment Carly got in the car.

"I think I could live to see a hundred years and still never be ready for this," she replied.

"Any more phantom messages? Last night I watched my Life360 obsessively. Mystery Mitch left the Roadside at around eight o'clock, poof, just like that, gone."

"You wouldn't believe me if I told you," Carly said. She didn't tell her sister that Mitch's departure tracked right at the same time she'd fled her room.

"Carls, it's not that I don't believe you. It's just that I find it hard to believe Father is reaching out to you from the unknown."

"Until I can prove it is someone among the living, I'll believe it is Mitch. He says he was murdered and apparently I'm supposed to do something about it."

Coffees in hand, the Bennett sisters made their way downtown to Mitch's attorney's office.

"Don't you look spiffy," Liv said as Carly got out of the car.

"You clean up pretty good yourself," Carly replied.

"I hid a spit-up stain under my scarf, and I'm hoping my Spanx and breast pads hold up their end of the bargain," Liv said as she opened the large leaded glass door. "Pun intended, wink-wink."

Carly felt she'd stumbled into another place and time upon entering the law office. An ornate pressed-tin ceiling was held up by more polished and carved woodwork than she'd ever seen. What appeared to be a walk-in humidor spanned one side of the luxurious foyer. Across the room, a receptionist sat behind a massive desk.

"May I help you ladies?" the receptionist asked with an air that said she believed Carly and Liv had come to the wrong place.

Liv strode to the desk with a confidence Carly could never emulate.

"Olivia Murphy and Carly Bennett, here to see Mr. Charles Childers."

"Oh, yes. The entire family is waiting in the conference room. Follow me," the receptionist said.

She led Carly and Liv down a long hallway, also encased in carved wood, trim, molding, doors; everything looked to be handcrafted and very expensive.

The receptionist paused before opening the door to the conference room and Liv did something that was shocking, even for Liv.

"You seem to be mistaken regarding the family. As Mitch Bennett's eldest daughters, the entire family has not arrived until we take our seats. Be a doll, please," Liv said, handing the receptionist her empty coffee cup.

Carly was glad she'd left her coffee in the car and smiled sweetly as the receptionist opened the heavy conference room door.

"Eldest?" Carly whispered.

"I don't know what came over me," Liv replied.

"Well, how nice of you girls to show up," Janace said. The woman sat closest to the lawyer. If she'd been any closer, she would be in his lap.

"To be fair, Mrs. Bennett," Mr. Childers said, "your brood arrived a bit early. Ms. Bennett and Mrs. Murphy are right on time. Please, have a seat, ladies."

"I thought the two of you might have been waiting outside for the doors to open like Black Friday shoppers," Chip stated, venom in his voice.

Kimmi fixed Chip with a look and hissed, "Really, Chip?" through clenched teeth.

"Well, bless your little heart, Chipper. Right out of the gate, huh? Thinking about Carly and me on a day like today, you're so sweet. I was just out shopping for that Lamborghini I've always wanted, and Carly was trying to decide which Rolex to buy."

Carly held her breath, hoping Chip would pipe down. The last thing this meeting needed was for Liv to lose her cool and announce to the expecting father he was not the actual father.

Liv smiled at Chip and took a seat next to him.

"Well, now that we're all here, shall we begin, Mr. Childers?" Janace asked, honey dripping from her words.

"Certainly," Mr. Childers replied, rising from his seat. "Inside the folder in front of you is the last will and testament of Mitchell Jacob Bennett. Now, I don't know what you were expecting today, but I haven't read a will out loud to a group of people since I don't know when. So, I've highlighted the details that pertain to each of you. Mr. Watts is here as he was witness to the final deed for Mr. Bennett." Mr. Childers motioned with his hands to a person sitting at the far end of the long table.

Carly was taken aback when she saw that Uncle Mark was also in the room.

"Mark, be a dear and scooch on down the table here. You're family, after all, maybe not in name, but in our hearts."

"Thank you, Janace, but I am fine right here," Uncle Mark replied.

"Suit yourself," Janace quipped before turning her attention to Mr. Childers. "This document is full of legal jargon. I think my head might pop off."

"That's what I am here for. You take as much time as you need, and I can answer any questions."

The room was eerily quiet for the next half hour as each of Mitch's bequeathed scoured the dossier.

Carly held out as long as she could before scanning the pages in search of her name. Throughout her life, she'd never envisioned being mentioned in her father's will. It wasn't until Liv said the man had called her and asked specifically what was expected that she'd entertained the idea she might receive something, not a financial windfall necessarily, but perhaps enough to go back to school. She hoped to study creative writing, not marketing, as some might assume. She'd never told anyone her dreams of writing a book. Being awarded a stake in any of Mitch's business ventures or any of his property wasn't on her wish list. But a little nest egg to put toward her education would be more than she'd ever hoped for.

She willed her hands to stop shaking, urged her feet to stop tapping, as her eyes fell on her name. Two hundred and fifty thousand dollars would be hers. Her entire body tingled, and tears leaked from her eyes.

A sharp gasp escaped Liv's mouth as she squeezed Carly's leg under the table. Carly saw the two were on the same page of the document. Half a million dollars between the two of them was almost unbelievable. She didn't care how much more Kimmi and Chip received. This amount of money was life-changing for her, even if it was merely chump change to Janace's children.

Janace cleared her throat before speaking. "I believe I understand most of this. Mitch left me our house and a one-quarter stake in his business ventures, along with his life insurance and stock holdings—"

"That is correct," Mr. Childers responded.

"Chip and Kimmi are the other recipients of their father's business holdings..."

"And a healthy sum of money."

"Yes, yes, two hundred fifty thousand each. But I'm confused by these words: intangible property, rest and residue."

"Stated simply, you, Chip and Kimmi are bequeathed an

equal share of Mitch's intangible property, which are the businesses Mitch owned. You, as his spouse, receive the rest and residue, for example, things like jewelry, his wedding ring, furniture, cars, etc."

Even learning of the plenitude Mitch left for his other kids didn't take the wind out of Carly's sails. She was content despite the disparity.

"I'm also confused about all this grandchild stuff."

"Your husband provided college fund trusts. Kimmi is the custodian of her children's trusts."

"Yes, yes, I see the names of the grandchildren, but there's no mention of Chip's unborn child," Janace stated.

"No mention of Liv's children either, just saying." Liv cupped her hand over her mouth and threw the words sideways under her breath. Carly hoped she was the only one to hear her sister's comment.

"I can tell by the date on this document that Mitch was well aware of the impending birth of his only son's son. I can't image he would have left that child out of the will. And wait, if I get one-fourth of the businesses, and Kimmi and Chip get one-fourth, that's only three. Who gets the other quarter?"

"The terms related to the child Rachel is carrying are on a different page." Mr. Childers drew the word out as he flipped through the document. "Here it is." He slid the packet to Janace, tapping his finger to indicate what she should read.

It was quiet for a moment, then Janace looked up from the paperwork. A look of disbelief etched on her face as her eyes fell on Mr. Childers before locking on to Rachel's.

"Chip's unborn child receives the remaining fourth of the business stakes?" Kimmi questioned, her expression one of bewilderment.

Mr. Childers cleared his throat. "Yes, those were Mr. Bennett's wishes."

"So, because Chip is a male heir, his kid gets a portion of the businesses and my kids get college funds? That's insane!"

Kimmi fumed. She was flipping through the pages, searching for verification.

"Now, Kimmi," Janace began.

"No, Mother, don't 'now Kimmi' me! Of all the sexist, pathetic ... I can't even!"

Liv removed her reading glasses and cleaned them. As she put them back on, she whispered to Carly.

"Needed to clean my glasses so I can help Kimmi find the gift horse's mouth."

Carly used an elbow jab to admonish her sister while stifling a laugh.

While Kimmi threw her tantrum, Carly saw that Chip wasn't focused on the conversation. His attention was on the will; he used his finger as a guide as he scanned the words. Next to him, Rachel sat calmly, her expression emotionless.

"Kimmi, you need to control yourself right now," Janace pleaded with her daughter.

Carly saw pure panic in Janace's eyes. She knew why Rachel's baby was bequeathed more than Kimmi's kids. Mitch's bold move could be a catalyst for the truth coming out, especially if Kimmi kept pushing the subject.

"No! I really can't believe he did this."

"Mrs. Jacobs," Mr. Childers interrupted. "I should inform you that your father insisted on a no-contest clause."

"Nonsense! I will be contesting it all right!" Kimmi's face was red. She gathered her things and stood, snatching her jacket from the back of her chair.

"What is a no-contest clause, Mr. Childers?" Janace asked.

"It basically states that if a party contests the will, they forfeit their inheritance."

Upon hearing the words, Kimmi slowly slunk back into her seat. A look of pure defeat softened her face as the color drained. She began to cry. Rachel pushed a box of tissue sitting on the table closer to her sister-in-law.

Carly realized she was smiling, watching the uproar as if it were a tennis match, her head bobbing back and forth. She would never admit it to anyone, but she found this meeting to be the best part of her trip home, and not just because of the money.

"Look," Mr. Childers began, sliding his finger into his shirt collar. "I suggest you all take some time to process the information. It is a lot to take in. Sleep on it. You might see things differently tomorrow."

"Great advice, Charles," Uncle Mark said, standing up.

Carly had forgotten Uncle Mark was there.

"Congratulations to you all," Uncle Mark said, moving toward the door. "I hope you enjoy your windfall ... with gratitude." His gaze fell on Kimmi, who huffed and crossed her arms. Uncle Mark left the conference room.

"Thank you, Mr. Childers, for your guidance. It is much appreciated," Janace said, rising and shaking the lawyer's hand.

"You're very welcome, Mrs. Bennett. My assistant will be in touch with all of you soon to make arrangements for financial transfers. Should you have any questions, I'm a phone call away. I'm very sorry for your loss. Mitch will be missed."

Chip rose from his seat and offered a hand to his wife, helping her up. Her belly had grown just since Carly had been in town. Carly wondered when her due date was. She also wondered if the life growing inside of Rachel would bring happiness or havoc to Janace and her children.

"Kimmi, let's go," Janace said.

Chip, Rachel and Mr. Childers shook hands. Kimmi rose and didn't say a word as she stomped out of the room.

Carly and Liv remained seated until the others departed.

"Let's give them a few minutes so they don't jump us in the parking lot," Liv said.

"Did either of you have any questions?' Mr. Childers asked as he gathered his papers.

"None that I can think of. Carly?" Liv replied.

"Um, no, I think I'm good. Thank you so much, Mr. Childers."

"You're very welcome, ladies."

Liv and Carly left the room.

In the car, Liv slammed her hands on the steering well and leaned forward.

"Woo, that was something," she said, her head buried between her arms. She looked up, a wide smile spread across her face. "We're rich, Carls!"

"We are, aren't we? Honestly, I never imagined he'd leave us a dime. Pleasant surprise is a massive understatement."

"Should we go shopping?" Liv asked.

"Well, the money isn't in our hands yet. Would you settle for lunch?

"Fine," Liv replied, rolling her eyes. "You're such a buzzkill sometimes. But I am starving. Apparently inheriting a vast sum of money works up an appetite! There's a great Japanese place on Main, Miso. Their chicken katsu is to die for."

Chapter Twenty-Two

2022

The lunch crush was in full swing at Miso, but the hostess found the Bennett sisters a secluded two-top table.

"Trust me on the katsu. It's the only thing I ever order here," Liv told Carly.

"I'm sold. Two chicken katsu it is."

"We need a celebratory drink. It isn't every day the Bennett sisters become quarter-millionaires," Liv said as she perused the spirits menu. "I found one, so fitting for today."

Liv ordered double katsu. "We'll take the Empress drink times two as well, please," she told the waitress.

"So, have you told Derek yet?" Carly asked.

"No, I'm trying to think of some clever way to give him the news. He's in surgery right now, so he hasn't been bombarding me with texts. What are you going to do with your share?"

"I'm going back to school. Don't make fun. It's something I've always wanted to do."

The server arrived with the drinks.

"Perfect! Maybe you'll find yourself a nice younger college

cutie in the desert, or a hot professor. At your age, it could go either way." Liv prodded.

"Maybe," Carly said, taking a long draw from the straw. "Good choice here on the drinks. Go slow though. You're a lightweight these days, and I don't want you to make a scene. How about you? What will the Murphy clan do with the money?"

"It's a toss-up. We really should pay our student loans off, but I've wanted to remodel the kitchen and bathroom since we bought our house. And there's that honeymoon we never took. So I'm not sure what will win out."

Once the food arrived, Liv leaned into the meaty topic they'd both been wanting to discuss.

"I was a little concerned about you being in the same room with Janace. Last night you were accusing her of murder. Did your feelings on her criminal status soften overnight?"

"I don't know. My rational mind tells me she would never do something so horrible. There's a tiny little voice reminding me of all the underhanded things she's done, and then there's some wacko out there harassing me via text insisting that Father was murdered. I can't let it go because something isn't allowing me to let it go."

"I don't know why she'd murder him over the will. She'll be just fine for the remainder of her days. It's almost as if nothing changes for her, except she sleeps alone."

"True, but have you seen her cry once since Mitch died? I mean, not at the funeral, not today. That's pretty cold."

"You and I know there's no cookie-cutter way to mourn, Carls. And to be fair, we aren't with her very often."

"Then there's the cremation. I don't get it. He was adamant about not being cremated. Best way I can think of to make certain there is no murder investigation is by making sure there's no body."

"Maybe we'll never know—"

"Are you okay with that? With not knowing if the woman murdered her husband? Would you feel safe letting your kids around someone who killed someone they supposedly loved?"

"Let's be honest here. My kids will never see Janace again unless they run into her in public. Mitch was our only link to that family and even when he was alive, we saw him at Christmas and birthdays maybe forty percent of the time. I can sleep just fine if Janace is a murderer because I get to wash my hands of her."

"That's one way to look at it. I don't know. Until I find out who is behind the text messages and social media posts, I may have no choice but to pursue the truth. You wouldn't believe what happened in my hotel room last night."

Liv put a piece of chicken in her mouth and nodded to Carly to carry on.

"I slept in the lobby."

Liv choked on her food, or more likely Carly's words, and took a healthy swig of her drink to wash it down.

"In the lobby? By choice?"

"Yes, Liv! I'm telling you, whether it's Mitch Bennett's ghost or not, someone wants something revealed and they've decided I am the one to do the revealing. All I want to do is go home and start picking my fall schedule."

"Sorry, Carls," Liv said. She pushed her drink to Carly. "You're going to have to take over that from here on; I've got to drive. I know I haven't been very supportive, it's just so far-fetched."

"I know more than anyone how far-fetched it is. But knowing doesn't keep it from happening."

The two ate their meals in silence for a while.

"You know, what if the problem Janace had with the will was because of how Rachel's baby was addressed? I mean, Mitch basically laid the secret of that poor child's paternity out on the table. I'm sure Janace would go to great lengths to keep that skeleton deep inside the closet."

"Yeah, she needs Kimmi to drop her hissy fit. Think she'd off Kimmi?" Carly asked with a laugh.

"Please! She'd jump in front of a train for her daughter. I'm sure Janace can devise something to sidetrack Kimmi."

"There's always Uncle Mark to look at," Carly suggested, keeping a close eye on her sister for her reaction.

"Back to Uncle Mark, huh? What could he possibly have to gain from Mitch being dead?"

"I don't know. He and Janace seem chummy these days. I did see the two of them at the no-tell motel. Maybe he wanted Mitch out of the way so he could be with Janace." Carly shivered as she said the words.

"You're forgetting one thing ... Aunt Char. They've been together longer than even Mitch and Janace. He loves her."

"I'm not denying his love. But Char has health problems. Maybe the stress of it all—"

"Carly, that's enough. You're really reaching now. Oh, I got a text!" Liv said, opening her phone. "Derek is out of surgery. He wants an update. I should do something special. Flowers? Balloons? Singing telegram?"

"I think the words themselves are special enough," Carly replied.

"You're right, but I should do it in person," Liv said as she flagged the waitress down for the check. "Mind if I drop you off at the Roadside first? I mean, you okay being alone?"

"I am totally fine with being alone."

Chapter Twenty-Three

2022

Carly cautiously entered her motel room. She was pleased to see that Marlow had freshened the room nicely. Besides clean bedding and towels, the trash bins were emptied, the toiletries replenished, and he'd done it all without changing the frigid thermostat setting. He had turned the lights off, so she went about the room turning them all back on as she waited for Bennett Automotive to answer her call.

She held her breath, hoping the news was good. She'd done what she came to do. Now that the will was revealed, she was ready to go home.

"No ma'am, it hasn't arrived yet, but I checked the tracking. It says it is out for delivery. Getting pretty late in the day, though. If it shows up before closing, we'll be sure to get your car on the schedule for first thing tomorrow morning. Barring any unforeseen trouble, it could be ready to pick up tomorrow afternoon."

"Well, that's something," Carly replied, not hiding her disappointment. "Thanks for the update, Trevor. Have a good one." She hung up the phone and got out of her dress, changing into jeans and a T-shirt, then flopped down on the freshly made bed. As she lay there replaying the day's events, her eyes got heavy. This bed was considerably more comfortable than the old sofa in the lobby. She allowed herself to drift off, no doubt aided by the Empress and a half she'd had at lunch.

When she woke, she grabbed her phone to check the time. She'd been asleep for over four hours. "Guess I needed that," she said to the empty room.

She had her leftovers from Miso in the mini fridge, but she wasn't yet hungry. From the bed, she flipped through the channels on the television when there was a knock on her door.

Carly pulled the curtains back just enough to see who knocked. It was Uncle Mark. He spotted Carly and waved. She had to let him in now. She smoothed her hair and opened the door.

"Hey, kiddo, how you holding up?" He removed his cowboy hat as he entered the room.

"Fine, all things considered. It's been a day."

"Certainly has," he agreed.

"Have a seat," Carly said, pointing to the chair before sitting on the bed and folding her legs under her. "What brings you here, Uncle Mark?"

He sat and sighed deeply.

"Carly, there's something I need to tell you. You can decide what to do with the information, but it's been weighing on me heavily."

"Okay, you're kind of scaring me, Uncle Mark."

"Think I scared myself with this one. What I did just wasn't me. I'm not sure how I let myself be talked into it. But you know, the more I try to put the pieces together, the more I realize I've done wrong."

"I'm listening," Carly replied, alarm bells going off in her mind.

"A while back, Janace told me Mitch was having some health issues. Actually, said he'd been having seizures. Now she claimed to be very concerned for the man but said no matter what she tried, she couldn't convince Mitch to see a doctor."

"Mitch? Seizures? Is that something related to his dementia?"

"Don't rightly know. But I started believing that Janace was making it all up. It was nothing overt. I spent time with your father. He didn't mention seizures. Seemed like the picture of health. But Janace pressed on. She suggested I let her try some of Char's meds. Poor woman has been given so many pills since her stroke; some work, others don't. They don't take them back if they prove useless. You just hold on to them and they clog up your medicine cabinet, but what are you going to do? They cost an arm and leg even with insurance. Dang pharmacy kept right on refilling the stuff. I was fielding so many doctors, therapists, treatments and such I never sorted through it all. I figured if the pills weren't helping my Char, they might help Mitch. I handed them over."

A few pieces fell together in Carly's mind like a puzzle. There were still too many bits missing for any of it to make sense. Uncle Mark pressed on.

"Now see, here's where it starts to get weird. After I gave Janace the pills, Mitch started getting worse. I didn't think anything of it at first. Really just believed that he couldn't hide the symptoms any longer."

"Did you ask him how he was?" Carly said, getting up from the bed and pacing the room.

"Well, sure. I mean guys rarely jump to seizures and forgetfulness right off the bat. But Mitch was a proud man. He wasn't prone to showing signs of weakness."

"That tracks. When did you say this all started?" Carly asked.

"Couple of years ago. Now, I know Mitch wouldn't have

wanted to burden me. I was going through a lot with Char. I asked Janace how he was doing. Everything she said fit the bill. He could relay any story from years ago like it'd happened yesterday, but couldn't remember from one minute to the next why he'd gone into another room, or tell you what he had for breakfast. Janace said he'd sometimes forget the names of his own kids. She'd have to show him old pictures to jog his memory."

"So why do you think Janace was drugging Mitch with medicines that didn't belong to him and didn't seem to help?"

"Only after he passed, I started to wonder the same thing."

"You remember the name of the medicine?" Carly asked, trying her best to sound nonchalant.

"Oh, I don't know, started with a K. Keppers, something of the sort. There's an ad on television, people dancing around and singing as if seizures were something to celebrate. Those pharmacy companies are always slinging something. Most times, they make it sound like the cure might be worse than the disease, so many side effects."

Carly struggled to keep her composure. She decided to keep her cards close to her chest.

"It's those side effects that got me thinking even more. Turns out, if you give someone some medicines they don't need, the side effects can be more pronounced, brutal even. One look at the fine print on that pill bottle told me all of Mitch's symptoms could be caused by the drug itself. Maybe he wasn't sick at all."

"Why did you do it, Uncle Mark?" Carly wasn't certain she'd get a straight answer, but the man seemed to be forthcoming with details and he obviously felt bad.

"I wanted to help him. Despite the way he treated you and your sister and his bullish attitude, we go way back. He's been my best friend since I can remember."

Carly saw a tear slip down the man's face. She fought the urge to hug him, still unclear of his motives.

"Uncle Mark, do you think Janace could have caused Mitch's death? Could she have given him too much of that medicine?"

"Oh, heck no, Carly," he replied. "Besides, she gave me back the unused pills. I don't think she has something that evil in her."

"I don't know about that," Carly mumbled. "So why then?"

"I think maybe it had to do with the will. Like she was trying to muddle his mind so he couldn't make any changes or rewrite the whole dang thing. But he did rewrite it. I was the witness. Childers didn't ask about Mitch's state of mind. The man appeared perfectly lucid. Who knows, maybe he caught on to Janace's tricks. She said she just told him they were vitamins. Maybe he suspected something and stopped taking them. I don't know."

"Were Liv and I in the will before those changes?"

"Ah, now, Carly. I hoped that wouldn't come up. You know I didn't agree with the way things were all these years. Man treated you like second-class citizens, your own father. But you know, I hate to make excuses for him. I think he was just too busy. Janace took care of the kids and pretty much everything. Figure she pulled the wool over his eyes countless times, and he was content to keep his head buried in the sand. Life was easier that way."

"No, that wasn't it. He just didn't care. Maybe it was because he was too busy, but do you know how hard it was for me and Liv? He abandoned us. He left us with a drug-addled woman. He had the power to lift us out of that life. He didn't. Uncle Mark, I need to know if we were in the will. From your reply, it sounds as if we weren't." Carly sat back down on the bed.

"So he added the funds for you and Liv and he changed

something else. Changed all that stuff about Chip's baby. Didn't really think much of it at the time. But you think Kimmi was right? Did Mitch leave more to Chip's son because he was a boy?"

"He never hid his disappointment about having all girls until he was graced with a son."

"Sure didn't. That's how he came up with the name. Chip off the old block," Uncle Mark said. Carly said the words with him in her best Mitch Bennett voice. "Maybe he wanted to make sure the business stayed in the family beyond Chip."

"Maybe," Carly said, her voice distant, her mind spinning. She was unwilling to reveal the real reason Chip's son was bequeathed more.

"Truth be told, that boy'll run at least half of those businesses into the ground within a year. It's a shame. Mitch worked hard to build his empire. Even if that empire was made up of mom-and-pops in a small college town. Every dad-gum thing those two have is on account of Mitch."

"Thanks for coming clean, Uncle Mark. Although that seems too harsh. You should quit beating yourself up. You thought you were helping; not like you could predict Janace's motives."

"Glad that's how you see it. I really didn't mean harm, but I know what I did broke a few laws according to the FDA and such. If you feel the need to talk to law enforcement, I understand."

"No, no, Uncle Mark. Your secret is safe with me. I would never throw you to the wolves over an act of kindness."

"An ill-conceived act of kindness, I'd say," he replied. He rose and took his hat from the table.

"Call it what you want, Uncle Mark. It's over now." Carly got up and crossed the room, embracing the man who she always wished could have been her father. A man who was not her blood, but who loved her more than her own. It felt good.

It felt right, and now Carly was crying right along with him. Uncle Mark squeezed her tightly.

"You're a good kid, Carly. Mitch didn't deserve you and your sister, and you certainly didn't deserve him."

"Thanks, Uncle Mark," she said, releasing him from the embrace. Carly walked him to the door, and he left.

She leaned back against the door after closing it. How had Janace kept all these secrets from everyone? She paced the room, going over everything she'd learned in the past few days. A notification pinged on her phone. She hoped it was Liv. How could she piece all of this together for her sister? There were still so many loose ends.

It wasn't Liv. It was Mitch.

FATHER: *You're so close.*

She tossed the phone onto the bed.

"No! I am not so close," she yelled. Before she'd finished her frustrated rant, the room was plunged into darkness. Her eyes hadn't adjusted to the absence of light when the television snapped on. First the Keppera ad, but it was different. The cheerful, dancing actors now appeared crazed. Some wore makeup that made them look like sad clowns. The song they sang was confused, distorted, and rang with a twisted, echoing quality. Then it stopped.

Next up was the grainy, black-and-white video of Janace and Rachel entering the abortion clinic. In this version, Janace regarded the camera directly, her face deranged; her smile depraved.

Gruesome images flashed on the screen, replacing her stepmother's monstrous face. They were pictures from Janace's picket signs, all too repulsive for Carly to look at. She covered her eyes but couldn't block out the sounds. Sounds of crying infants, of traumatized women, of protesters hurling horrific condemnations to suffering people.

"Stop! Please, just stop!" she screamed. The sounds stopped. Next on the screen was an image she recognized immediately. It was the tipped-over trash can in Mitch and Janace's room the night of the funeral reception.

She stared at the image, moving closer to the screen. Her mind traveled back to that night. Closing her eyes, she fought to remember the room. It was clean, pristine even. Janace always spoke highly of her housekeepers. Carly had never seen so much as a crumb in the kitchen, a dust mote on the bookshelves, or a dish in the sink. So why was that trash bin left unemptied in the room? She opened her eyes again and fixated on the items that had fallen out.

Uncle Mark said Janace returned unused Keppera pills. If she'd overdosed him, she would have used everything she had. Why take the chance that there wasn't enough in his system to do him in? Nothing made sense.

The lights flickered and came on. One word flashed on the screen in a bloody scrawl: *MURDER*.

It was all too much for her to process and she collapsed on the bed, feeling as if all her energy had been syphoned away. The only thing she wanted was to be at home, in her own bed. She closed her eyes, hoping sleep would steal her away from the tangled mess that wouldn't let up. This wasn't her battle. There was no way she could care less about who or what killed her father. She longed to sleep. To simply sleep away the next few hours until she could flee this town and the menacing presence who threatened her sanity. It was no use. Despite her mental exhaustion, the late nap prevented her body from succumbing to her desire to dream it all away.

With a heavy sigh, she pushed herself up when an icy hand grabbed her wrist. The terror was crushing. Adrenaline surged inside her. She turned to find her father sitting on the bed with her. She wrenched her arm from his frigid grasp and fell off the bed. Mitch rose and turned to Carly. His face was ghastly, ashen blue, his eyes opaque and lifeless.

She scuttled away from him in an awkward backwards crab crawl until she bumped against the wall. Blindly and frantically, she searched for the door. When her hand found the doorknob, she rose on shaky legs, opened the door, and fled.

Outside, the darkness rushed her and the early spring chill wrapped itself around her. Carly knew she had to learn more. If she were to be free of this—whatever it was—haunting her, she had to get answers to all the questions. There was only one person she could think of who could answer them all. She ran to the motel lobby.

Iva sat behind the reception desk, reading a book.

"Oh, hey, Carly," she said. "How's it going?"

"Not good. Could I ask a huge favor?"

"Sure, shoot."

"I need to borrow your car. I'll pay you, plus give you gas money. I just really need to get somewhere right now and my car is still in the shop."

Before Carly had finished explaining, Iva was digging through her backpack. She pulled her car keys out and handed them to Carly.

"Sorry," Iva said. "The stereo doesn't work, but other than that, the old thing is pretty reliable."

"Thank you, thank you, thank you! I owe you!" Carly said as she left the lobby.

Chapter Twenty-Four

2022

Carly was always surprised how dark the back roads were on the way to Camelot Crossing. She wasn't surprised her instincts hadn't faltered. As she made her way down Range Road, she focused as much on what sat to the sides of the bumpy country lane as she did on the road itself. The deer were plentiful in this corner of Stillwater, not to mention opossums, raccoon, and armadillos. She'd driven the back roads of Stillwater countless times in her youth and managed to not end a critter's life; she wasn't about to riddle herself with the guilt of making roadkill out of something now on what she hoped would be the last time she'd travel this route.

Rounding the hairpin bend at the bridge, she didn't let her guard down. For every one animal on Range, there'd be four or more on the narrow lanes of the neighborhood.

Still, the dark night called out shadows that lurched from behind clusters of trees. Monsters in the shape of people she'd known all her life appeared in her headlights, emerging from the weed-choked culverts along the route. She knew it was her overworked mind that conjured these rogues and did her best to ignore the apparitions and focus on safely arriving at her destination, all the while understanding the dreadful scene that awaited her was far more treacherous than these imaginary demons.

A sublime scene greeted her as she turned into the cul-de-sac, each house aglow in meticulously designed landscape lighting. Floodlights, porch lights, pathway lights, even string lights gave the homes a most inviting warmth. It was like something out of a magazine. An ideal front that hid vile and ugly actualities.

Carly parked the car at the end of Janace's drive. Even before she exited the vehicle, she could hear the buzzing chirps of the katydid and the rattle of the cicada. The chatter amplified as she drew near the front door. She paused, took a deep breath, and reminded herself that this had to be done and it had to be done by her.

She rang the bell. Katia's high-pitched yapping pierced the night, almost drowning out the noisy insects.

Carly knew the wait could be long. It was an enormous house. Janace would no doubt check her doorbell camera before opening her door after dark. She remained patient, pushing back against the voice telling her to leave, that this was a fool's errand.

"Coming," Janace yelled. Carly could hear the woman's heels clicking on the marble floors of the foyer.

"Well, for heaven's sake, Carly," Janace complained as she opened the door. "What on earth are you doing here? Do you know how late it is?"

"Yes, Janace," she said, pushing past the woman who had not yet opened the door wide enough for Carly to pass. "This is very important. I really need to talk to you."

Janace closed the door and turned to Carly, scooping up the tiny dog as she did.

"I swear, if this is about that will, then you're barking up the wrong tree. Your father did that, and you heard what Mr.

Childers said about that no-contest gibberish. There's not a darn thing I can do about any of it."

"This has nothing to do with the will, Janace. Is there somewhere we can sit?"

"This is incredibly rude of you, Carly. Barging in here unannounced."

Carly was walking away from the woman, moving toward the family room. It was the only room lit. The muted lights of a television drew her in. She spotted a full wineglass on the side table of the couch and took the seat across from it.

"Well, I never! Just help yourself, young lady. Are you going to snatch my wine as well?" Janace said, trailing behind Carly.

Janace sat down and took a healthy swig of red wine. Katia tucked herself in between her owner and the arm of the couch, all but disappearing. Only a tuft of fur wrapped in a pink bow marked the dog's presence.

"You might need more of that before I'm done," Carly informed her.

"Clearly you have something on your chest that you need to unload, so let's just get to it. Of all the ... this late hour," Janace mumbled as she examined her manicure.

"Janace, did you kill Mitch?" Carly felt outside of herself, like her voice wasn't her own, and she wondered who was so bold as to ask the question outright.

"What the...? Seriously, Carly, have you lost your mind? Did I kill Mitch?"

"Well, did you?"

"I most certainly did not kill my husband." Janace rose and took a step toward Carly. "I think you need to excuse yourself."

"I'm not leaving until I get some answers. I know you were drugging him."

Carly's words collided with the woman, forcing her back

to the sofa. She nearly squashed her dog as she dropped to her seat.

"Drugging him?" Janace said before taking another drink of wine. Carly noted the glass was almost empty.

"Yes, drugging him. With Aunt Char's medications. Was he really having seizures, or did you just make that part up?"

Janace did not speak. She rose again and left the room. Katia rolled into the void her owner left. The dog stood, shook her whole body and peered at Carly, fixing her with a half-hearted snarl before resituating herself between the cushions. Carly remained in her chair and looked around the room. Janace had paused FOX News, presumably when she heard the doorbell. The talking head on screen was frozen in a comical expression that made her look as if she were about to sneeze.

Janace came back into the quiet den, the bottle of wine uncorked and in her hand. To Carly's surprise, she held an extra glass. She poured a healthy splash and set it on the table next to Carly before filling her own glass and taking her seat again.

"So, you've been talking to Mark," Janace said, not as a question but a statement. "I'm rather surprised he turned to you. Then again, he always had a fondness for you and your sister; I never understood it."

Janace was quiet. She picked an invisible piece of lint from her shirt and kicked off her heels. Carly waited in silence.

"I did give meds to Mitch, but I thought he needed them," she said when she finally spoke.

Carly could tell the woman's mind was pedaling fast, trying to keep ahead of the game. It was apparent Janace had never thought through this possibility, having to explain her actions. She hadn't yet devised a good story and was stalling. Carly interrupted her internal brainstorming session.

"So Mitch experienced seizures?"

"No, well—"

"Because he didn't need the medication if he wasn't."

"I know that. Carly, it's a long story and there's too many moving parts for me to rehash with you at this hour."

"I told you I wasn't leaving until I got answers," Carly said, her voice sharp with steely confidence.

"Well, there's where we have a problem. I don't have any answers for you, Carly. Other than no, I did not kill my husband."

"Maybe it was an accident? You gave him too much one night, or he mixed it with too much wine—"

"Your father didn't drink wine," Janace interjected.

"Janace, we can dance around the subject all night if you'd like," Carly continued. "If it was an accidental overdose, then why lie? Why not call for help?"

"He was cold when I found him, Carly." Janace finished the wine that remained in her glass, then wrapped her arms around herself. "It was too late for help. Truth is, I don't know what killed Mitch. Maybe he had a heart attack, maybe it was the virus. All I know is that I never gave him too much of anything, and he was beyond help when I found him."

Carly was shocked to see tears streaming down Janace's face. Her expression hadn't changed much at all, but she was crying. This was the first time Carly had ever seen the woman cry.

"So why the cremation? Why did you do that to him? You know that wasn't what he wanted."

"That was an act of self-preservation," Janace said, sitting up straight and brushing tears away. "I couldn't be sure if they'd want to run tests or not. I wasn't going to risk it. Despite voicing his aversion to cremation, he'd never issued a directive regarding his remains. As his wife, it was my prerogative."

"Surely you can see it makes you look all the more guilty, Janace."

"What do you want me to say, Carly?" Janace rose from

the couch, her voice shrill, her hands shaking. Katia, startled by the woman's sudden movement and tone, jumped off the couch, whimpering.

"What? That I killed my husband? If I say that, will you leave? Fine, then, fine." She was quiet and moved to the window. Katia fled the room, leaving behind a puddle on the wood floor. "Mitch was going to change the will. He told me he was going to, but wouldn't tell me what changes he was making. So I tried to figure out a way to make him look incompetent. You can learn a lot from those pharmaceutical commercials."

She tossed her head over her shoulder and delivered the last line directly at Carly. Harsh black rivers of mascara cut through her pale face. She ran a hand through her hair, the act rendering her coiffed style unkempt and wild.

"It was genius, really, if I do say so myself," she laughed, the sound caustic. "Just didn't work the way I'd planned, obviously."

Carly recoiled, pressing herself against the back of the overstuffed armchair.

"Make my husband look as if he was losing his faculties. Make sure he doesn't change his will. Make sure he doesn't push me out. I earned every bit of this!" she raged, spinning in a circle, arms raised as if in victory. The wine glass fell from her grip and shattered to the floor. She moved about the room, her fingers tracing a lampshade. She plucked a pillow from the sofa and squeezed it before tossing it aside. From the bookshelf she grabbed a vase and rotated in her hands, admiring the prism cuts, a look of wonder on her face. She placed it back on the shelf. But in an act that shocked Carly, she poked a finger at the crystal vessel and pushed it. It fell unceremoniously and splintered as it made contact with the floor.

"You think you and your sister are the only ones with less than ideal upbringings?"

Carly made to answer, but Janace continued before she could speak.

"Well, you're not. I came from nothing, less than nothing. My worthless mother was just like yours. Of all the kids she had, I was the only one unlucky enough to have not ended up in the system. I wasn't fortunate enough to end up in a foster home like the others. Lord knows I would have been better off if I had, but that's where I got this drive. I fought for a better life."

Janace delivered this bombshell while staring out the window into the darkness. She stood silently for a few minutes. It was almost as if she forgot her stepdaughter shared the room with her. But then she snapped to and turned in a rush.

"It's all mine, and I worked for it! I can do whatever I want with it now. It wasn't easy prying that man out of the pathetic grip of your strung-out mother." She drew close to Carly's face and hissed the words with bared teeth. Her remarks regarding Mother came at Carly like a slap to the face. The sweet wine on her breath made Carly nauseous. "So you can't come in here, into my domain, and act like I owe you anything!"

The lights, both indoor and out, flickered and then extinguished, hurling the women into darkness. A small yelp escaped Janace's mouth. The television flashed, and the image on the screen flip-flopped, settled and became clear. It was the footage that showed Janace escorting Rachel into the abortion clinic.

Janace said nothing, but lifted the bottle of wine to her mouth, draining its contents before turning her attention to the screen. Carly took her first sip and waited.

When the video clip ended, Janace spoke. "Where'd you get that? You think this is going to ruin me or something? Nice try. It proves nothing."

Neither of them heard the approaching footsteps until the woman walked into the room.

Chapter Twenty-Five

2022

"Rachel?" Carly couldn't conceal the shock of seeing her sister-in-law.

On the television, the video replayed. Rachel was drawn to the scene, eyes wide. She reached out with shaky hands and touched the screen.

"What is this, Carly?" Rachel said. "Janace, did you give her this? What's going on?"

"Of course I didn't give it to her. I have no clue how she got her hands on it. She thinks she's got some mind-bending piece of evidence here." Janace laughed.

"Where did you get this, Carly?" Rachel pleaded. She backed away from the television and almost fell into Carly's lap before righting herself and turning on her heels. "How? Who knows about this? Janace, you said no one would ever find out." Rachel's voice shook, the volume ratcheting up with each word.

"Nobody knows a thing," Janace replied. The woman swayed as she stood in the window. "Why is the power out?" she asked. "Why didn't the generator come on?"

"I actually know quite a bit about the two of you and your sordid secrets," Carly said.

"Oh, really? What is it you think you know, Carly?" Janace crossed the room and flipped the light switches off and on. The room remained shrouded in darkness.

"I, I—" Carly started. She listened to her own voice, disbelieving it was hers. "I know you didn't miscarry."

Janace and Rachel turned to look at Carly. They wore matching expressions. Thunderstruck.

"I know you aborted your baby, and I know why."

Rachel made a move toward Carly, her mouth moving but no sound coming out, as if she had much to say but couldn't find the words. Janace held out an arm and stopped Rachel's movement.

"Don't say a word!" Janace said. "She's bluffing."

Carly pushed on. There was no point in trying to back out now.

"Because the baby wasn't Chip's. It was Lance's." Carly said it and then sat back, biting her lip.

A growling scream rose from Rachel, and she turned toward Janace.

"You told her?" She grabbed Janace's shoulders and shook her. The woman's hair tossed about. "How dare you? We said we'd take it to our graves! Do you know the lengths I've gone to protect this, this unspeakable thing?"

Janace freed herself from Rachel's grip and slapped her hard across the face. Carly was watching both women come undone.

"You shouldn't have been with him! Of all the people you could have chosen from, you picked my daughter's husband? That's on you, Rachel!"

Rachel held her palm to her face, her cheeks wet with tears, and crumpled onto the couch.

"She said she wouldn't let me muddy the waters," she said, her speech trance-like. "Told me I couldn't keep the baby, but promised me something in return. Her? Of all people, she took me to the clinic. The same clinic she's picketed for years and forced me to do the very thing she fought to abolish. How does she do that? Muddy the waters?"

"Stop!" Janace exploded. "You stop talking right now!"

Carly felt like an outsider eavesdropping on a preposterous conversation, much like she and Liv did at the hospital. Try as she might, she couldn't connect all the dots and reluctantly interfered.

"Why couldn't you just have Chip's baby? Why did you turn to Lance? Were you having an affair?"

"Don't, Rachel," Janace protested before Rachel could speak.

"Oh, you don't know that part?" Rachel offered a defeated laugh. "The part about her precious Chip being sterile." She now held her finger to her lips and fixed Carly with a wide-eyed stare. "Shooting blanks. All because of a football injury when he was a child. And Janace has kept that little secret hidden away for years. She hid it from me for a long time. Watched me struggle, thinking I was infertile. It wasn't until I told her I'd made an appointment at a fertility clinic, she let me know. She knew Chip wanted a baby as badly as I did and recommended I discreetly secure a pregnancy outside my marriage. Swore Chip wouldn't be any the wiser."

Carly was rendered speechless, but finally a few more pieces of the chaotic puzzle snapped into place.

"I wasn't having an affair with Lance. We were together once. One time, when the rest of them went on a cruise. Lance and I couldn't take the time off work, so we were stuck here. Just the two of us. By then I was desperate for a child, and the opportunity fell into my lap. The guilt was overwhelming, and we swore to never do it again. But a funny thing happened. After years of trying for a child with my husband, I was suddenly pregnant." Rachel rubbed her growing belly as she spoke.

"That's enough, Rachel," Janace said, approaching the woman, arms stretched out. It looked as if she would hug the pregnant woman. "You should go lie down, dear. You look exhausted." Janace's voice was now syrupy.

Rachel stood and shoved Janace, nearly causing her to topple over. Janace recovered and sat on the sofa.

"You're right, Janace," Rachel continued. "I am exhausted. It's exhausting keeping all your nasty little secrets hidden."

Carly leaned in hard, determined to understand.

"So Chip doesn't even know he's unable to father a child?" she asked.

Rachel laughed the laugh of someone who was unhinged.

"Would you like to field that question, Janace?" She waited for Janace to respond. "No, okay, I'll take this one too. The answer is no, my husband has no idea that he can't procreate. She never told him. Didn't want to injure his pride. Naturally, he was ecstatic when I announced my pregnancy." Rachel went to the window, her figure a mere silhouette in the absence of light. She stood in silence for some time.

"But this one," she said, turning and pointing a finger at Janace. "This one here wouldn't let up. Constantly questioning me, clawing for the identity of the man who got me pregnant. I caved. I told her it was Lance and, well, things got ugly."

"I think we've all had enough of this," Janace said. "It's late. Why are you dragging skeletons out? It isn't helping anything."

"Oh, you want me to stop? You'd like that, wouldn't you, Janace? Well, I'm tired of being quiet. Carly should know who she is dealing with."

Carly wanted to say that she'd known what Janace was capable of for a long time, but kept quiet.

"That's when she said I had to abort it. Told me she'd tell everyone what I'd done. All I wanted was to be a mother. I didn't want to leave Chip, didn't want to betray Kimmi. I just wanted a baby."

Rachel was crying again. Her hands massaged her stomach. Self-soothing, Carly supposed.

"That baby would have destroyed this family!" Janace shrieked. "My daughter would have been the aunt and the stepmother of that forsaken mistake. You forced my hand!"

"She wasn't a mistake, Janace. She was a life. A life growing inside of me. My body! I loved that baby. You took her, Janace! You took her life! Go ahead and tell her who the father of this baby is. Tell her. Tell her how you kept it in the family, ensured a pure bloodline." Rachel's eyes had been fixed on Janace, but now she turned to Carly. "Brace yourself, Carly. This one is a doozy."

Though Carly knew the paternity of Rachel's baby, she kept her mouth shut. If she filled in the blanks for Janace and Rachel, she might miss out on other hidden details.

"Cat got your tongue, Janace? But you were so proud of your plan. Said it was foolproof. Guaranteed I'd never be tossed aside when Chip tired of me like Mitch tired of your mother, Carly. Promised me I'd always be taken care of. She offered me…" Rachel paused, her shoulders hitched as she was overcome with sobbing. The room was silent while Rachel fought to regain her composure. "She offered me her own husband." Rachel spit the words out of her mouth as if the words themselves tasted foul.

"Rachel, you make it sound so tawdry. I was merely trying to help. Everyone got what they wanted."

"Is that what you tell yourself, Janace? That this—" She gestured to her belly as if it weren't a part of her. "This is what I wanted? What Chip wanted? That Chip would be fine raising his own brother as his child? Do you hear how that sounds? It is beyond tawdry! It's vile, sadistic!"

Janace hung her head, shaking it as if she could make Rachel's words evaporate. Rachel kept on.

"You're not the only one with secrets though, Janace. I've been keeping a few juicy tidbits from you. Get this. Your husband fell in love with me. Isn't that rich? Your faithful Mitch told me all this could be mine if I loved him in return. As if!"

Janace lifted her head and regarded Rachel with disbelief.

"That's right. He said he was in love with me. Even suggested he leave you. Where would that have left you? Tossed aside like yesterday's garbage."

"He would never," Janace insisted.

"Oh, yes, he would! Are you listening, Carly?"

Carly nodded. She was shocked either of them remembered she was still in the room.

"Because here's where it gets really twisted. I can play your demented little games as well, Janace. Me, quiet little Rachel, quiet Rachel who can never stand up for herself, that same Rachel took things into her own hands. Mitch was going to tell Chip. He wanted to tell the world that he'd done it again. He was bringing another son into the world. I wasn't going to let that happen. Couldn't let it happen."

Janace looked at Rachel. Her face spoke of an understanding. She seemed to know what Rachel would say next.

"It was easy. He was sick. I played the devoted nursemaid to perfection. You were off making sure other women lost control of their own destinies, self-righteously fighting for unborn children. You valued other people's fetuses more than mine!" Halting sobs made it difficult for Rachel to continue. She choked out the words, gasping for air. She sat again, and held her head in her hands, crying uncontrollably for what seemed like minutes. Neither Carly nor Janace moved. Carly was holding her breath, waiting for someone to continue. The heinous actions perpetrated by her own family members were snowballing into something inconceivable.

"I brought everything with me that I needed. I'd gathered the items from different stores, paid cash. All perfectly legal, eye drops and nose spray. Common commodities in the pandemic era. No one would bat an eye. Filled the Gatorade bottle with my secret recipe. He drank it down without a care. He couldn't taste anything at that point."

Janace sat motionless. Her mouth hanging open, her hands shaking. Carly wished she could skulk out of the room and into the night. The information she had now was dangerous. Rachel was clearly capable of things no one would imagine.

"The only surprise to me was how fast it went. I expected a long night, even considered that I might have to hold a pillow over his face to wrap it all up, but no. He made it so simple. I held on to the trash bin that contained all my evidence and put it back in your room, Janace. Part of me wished you'd get caught for my crime. I wanted so badly to see you dig yourself out of that mess. But something interfered with that. I think you know what I'm talking about, Carly."

"What, me? No, Rachel. I don't have a clue—"

"Hey, it's fine. We're all sharing secrets tonight." Rachel's voice took an eerie calm that gave Carly the chills. "He's been contacting you too, hasn't he?"

"Who?" Carly whispered.

"Why, Mitch silly. He's been messing with my head from the moment he took his last breath. Texting me. Condemning me for my actions. I could see it in your eyes at the service. Mitch was working on you, too."

"I don't know what you're talking about, Rachel." Carly was certain she didn't want to share anything with either of these women ever again. All she wanted to do was get out of there. The truth was more ghastly than she ever could have guessed.

"That's fine. I, of all people, understand if you want to keep some things to yourself. So what next, Carly? Guess you'll drive straight to the police. Have me arrested for murdering your father?"

Though given no time to mull over her next move, Carly knew exactly how to answer this question.

"Not at all, Rachel." Carly rose and pulled Iva's car keys from her pocket. "I'll see myself out."

As Carly left the room, Janace chased after her, finally catching up with her in the entryway. Rachel followed.

"You can't just leave like this. How do we know you won't tell?" Janace implored.

"You two and the lives you've created are bad enough without the threat of a trial and imprisonment. But my reasoning goes deeper than that. My father could have rescued Liv and me from the life of poverty and uncertainty when we were young. He chose not to. My mother could have sought a fair life for Liv and me. She chose not to. I could have you arrested and seek justice for my father's death. I choose not to as well. Not to seek release for Mitch's spirit. Not to avenge his murder. Not to seek revenge on the two of you. I don't care about justice for any of you. I never deserved his time, and now he doesn't deserve mine. I am walking out of this house, and I hope to never see either of you again. The only thing that might change that is if you attempt in any way to drag Liv into your demented little soap opera. Leave her alone, and I'll leave you alone."

Carly turned, opened the door and walked out. As she made her way down the front walk, all the lights inside and outside of Janace's home came on.

Chapter Twenty-Six

2022

Carly awoke to the ringing of her phone. She groped for it and brought it to her face, expecting to silence the call. It was Bennett Automotive, so she answered.

"Good morning, Ms. Bennett," the voice said.

"It's Carly, Trevor. Good morning to you, too. Do you have good news for me?"

"I do. Your car is right as rain and ready to be picked up," Trevor replied.

"Oh, Trevor, I could hug you! I'll be in soon to settle up."

"Sounds good. See you soon."

She texted Liv and asked for a ride, then hurried around the room, gathering her belongings before taking a quick shower. Her bags were packed and waiting by the door with her when Liv arrived.

"Good morning. I'm sad," Liv said as Carly loaded her stuff into her sister's back seat. "Don't wake the beast." Little Asa was napping in his car seat.

Carly got in the front seat and whispered, "Good morning."

"You know I should just not take you to your car. Kidnap you and hold you for ransom. I don't want you to leave." Liv turned to Carly after pulling out of the Roadside parking lot and put on her best pouty face.

"I've got to get back to my life. I've got so much to do. I don't think I've been this excited in years."

"So, you aren't going to miss me?"

"Of course, I'll miss you! You need to bring the kids out to Arizona. Let them see what they're missing."

"Right, right, the dry heat and all," Liv joked.

At Bennett Automotive, Trevor was quick to get Carly back in her car. She drove to Liv's, hopefully squeezing in a nap before making the drive back to Tempe.

She pulled into Liv's driveway behind her and carried Asa's carrier into the house. The baby was still sleeping soundly.

"They plot this in their tiny little brains. Sleep the best while Mom is driving and can't accomplish anything other than, well, driving. He'll wake up the second I try to load the dishwasher or fold some laundry," Liv complained as they entered the house.

"Aunt Carly!" Fallon shouted. Asa stirred and let out a wail.

"Derek pulled a double shift but has graciously offered to take this little monkey for ice cream so we can talk," Liv said, scooping Fallon into her arms.

"Ice cream! Ice cream!" Fallon sang.

Derek entered the living room.

"Hey, Carls. Heading back to the desert today, huh?"

"Yep, kind of getting tired of hanging out with my favorite adorable little family."

"Hey." Liv slugged Carly's arm before freeing Asa from his car seat. She settled in and lifted her shirt to feed the boy, quieting his cries instantly.

"Ice cream! Ice cream!" Fallon continued.

"Yes, yes," Derek said. "You scream, then I scream and then everybody is just screaming and there's ice cream." Derek rolled his eyes and scooped Fallon up in his arms before drawing Carly in for a hug. From her position in his arms, Fallon hugged Carly's neck. "Be safe out there, sis," Derek said before releasing her.

He ushered Fallon out of the house. "Next stop: Blue Spruce!" he yelled as he galloped to the car with his daughter.

Carly closed the door and sat on the couch.

"There's something about you that seems different suddenly," Liv said.

"Maybe a good night's sleep? I've struggled with it since I got here."

"Maybe that's it, but I don't think so. Anything new from Impostor Mitch?" Liv covered herself and put Asa on her shoulder, gently patting his back.

"Um, no, not for a bit. He's been quiet."

"Convinced it is a he, huh?"

"Oh, I don't know. I haven't really given it much thought. But whoever it was, I think I've heard the last of it."

"That's good. Sorry if I gave you too much grief about the whole thing. Mourning can really mess with people."

"No worries," Carly said. She thought about asking Liv to steer clear of the other side of the Bennett family, but had a hunch the tattered relationship would wither on its own. She had never kept secrets from her sister. But the reality of what their father and Janace had done, the lengths Rachel had gone to, were all too heinous. The last thing Carly wanted to do was to burden her sister with the knowledge of such evil acts. Although she wasn't sure she would be able to keep it from Liv forever, for now she believed it best to keep it all buried.

"I think this one is full now, and he needs a diaper change," Liv said, handing Asa to Carly. "I'm going to go load that dishwasher."

"Do what you need to do. Don't mind me. I'll just mind this little guy," Carly cooed.

She took Asa to his room, changed him, and played with him for some time. When he seemed to have enough, she sat in the rocking chair and read a book to him. He nodded off in her arms. She propped her feet on the footstool and fell asleep.

When he woke, she took him back to Liv.

"He's hungry again."

The two women sat down so Liv could feed Asa, and the front door flung open.

"Aunt Carly, we got you some ice cream!"

"Yes, I love ice cream!"

"It's actually gelato, but whatever," Derek said, handing Carly a small cup and a plastic spoon.

"Where's mine?" Liv asked.

"I've got it right here," Derek said. "I'll put it in the freezer until you can eat it."

Carly ate dinner with the family and just before Fallon's bedtime, she said goodbye to them all. As usual, Liv cried, and Carly fought back tears. She double-checked her Bluetooth connection and plugged her phone in before driving away. Her stereo worked fine for the entire drive.

———

When Carly arrived back at her apartment, she was too road-wired to sleep. She grabbed her laptop and started searching for courses at ASU. Clovis curled up next to her, purring loudly. She grabbed the remote and turned the television on, hoping some background noise would drown out the ringing in her ears she got from the long drive.

On the television, a young Richard Dreyfus, dressed in chinos and a madras shirt, approached a young Ron Howard as he leaned against a white Chevy Impala. "Rock Around the Clock" played over the scene. Carly set her laptop on the coffee table, pulled a throw blanket around her and Clovis, and settled in to watch her father's favorite movie.

Acknowledgments

For this book, I have to acknowledge my siblings: Juli, Emily and Will. Though we each walked different and difficult paths, our bond remains strong. We survived, persevered and were steadfast in ensuring our children could never comprehend what we endured.

As always, much thanks to my family for tolerating me while I navigate this authoring realm. I appreciate your patience and support. Many, many, many thanks to Dar and my aunts!

Tremendous gratitude to Two Birds Author Services. Your guidance and expertise have been invaluable.

Lastly, thank you Kristin and my great friends in the SHS graduating class of 1986. Your support and encouragement have done wonders for my confidence. You will never know how grateful I am for having such a great cheering section!

About the Author

Lisa Courtaway lives in Stillwater, Oklahoma and is married with four children. An entourage of six dogs follows her everywhere. She has worn many career-hats, from advertising to insurance to education. Currently she is dreaming up her next story.

She loves a good ghost story, and has lived in several homes that spoke to her in mysterious ways. True crime stories, watching a binge-worthy series, reading, and lovingly meddling in the lives of her children are her favorites.

Since she was young, people have often told her she should write a book ... so she did ... and then did it again ... and again ... and she plans to keep doing so.

You can find out more about Lisa, including her social media links, and content at her website:

www.lisacourtaway.com